"Is our friendship a problem, Bay?"

"It's not a problem," Bay interrupted. "Meeting you has been the best thing that's happened to me… ever." Surprised by her own words, she sneaked a peek at David.

He looked straight ahead, but he was smiling. "I feel the same way," he told her quietly. "And I have to admit, I'm a little conflicted because—" He stopped and started again. "Because, well… Well, I'm just going to say it, Bay. If you were Mennonite, I'd ask you on a date."

For a moment, Bay was silent. Stunned.

But then she felt a warmth in the pit of her stomach. She had suspected he liked her—in that way—but she hadn't quite trusted her own instincts.

David groaned and gripped the steering wheel tightly. "I shouldn't have said that. I'm sorry. Totally inappropriate. I'm so sorry."

"You'd ask me out on a date?" she asked, feeling bold with newfound confidence.

She had been right!

He did like her…

Emma Miller lives quietly in her old farmhouse in rural Delaware. Fortunate enough to have been born into a family of strong faith, she grew up on a dairy farm, surrounded by loving parents, siblings, grandparents, aunts, uncles and cousins. Emma was educated in local schools and once taught in an Amish schoolhouse. When she's not caring for her large family, reading and writing are her favorite pastimes.

Visit the Author Profile page at LoveInspired.com for more titles.

Their Secret Courtship

Emma Miller

LOVE INSPIRED
INSPIRATIONAL ROMANCE

LOVE INSPIRED®
INSPIRATIONAL ROMANCE

Recycling programs
for this product may
not exist in your area.

ISBN-13: 978-1-335-56748-2

Their Secret Courtship

Love Inspired
22 Adelaide St. West, 41st Floor
Toronto, Ontario M5H 4E3, Canada
www.LoveInspired.com

Printed in U.S.A.

Two are better than one; because they have a good reward for their labour.

—*Ecclesiastes* 4:9

Chapter One

"Whoa, easy, Sassafras!" Bay murmured when the mare shied as a minivan laid on its horn and sped past them. The iron-wheeled wagon swayed ominously, but she held tightly to the reins and guided the dapple-gray back to the middle of the blacktop lane. She didn't understand how *Englishers* didn't know that beeping their horn could startle a horse, but she always tried to be charitable. Not everyone, she reminded herself, grew up with farm animals.

Bay let out a sigh of relief as Sassafras found a steady stride again, and she relaxed on the rough-hewn board that served as a bench seat. She'd been driving a horse and wagon since she was ten years old, but Sassafras was nearly thirty and more skittish than she once was. If Bay hadn't left in such a hurry, maybe she would have considered taking one of the surer-footed horses from her stepfather's barn. She gazed overhead at the dark clouds gathering and wished she hadn't acted so impulsively. Especially with a potential storm blowing in. But she'd been so eager to get away from her mother that she hadn't been thinking clearly when she decided to go into town for gardening supplies.

Gripping the leathers firmly in her hands, Bay gave Sassafras more rein, urging the mare into a faster trot as a rumble of thunder reverberated in the sky. The first raindrops began to fall. "Good girl," she soothed.

A disagreement with her mother was what had pushed Bay to get off the farm even knowing a storm might be coming in. She didn't need the supplies today; she'd just used that as an excuse to cut a conversation short with her mother. It was the same argument at least once a week, and she was tired of it. Ever since her twin, Ginger, had married last spring, their mother had been fussing about it being time for Bay to wed, too. At twenty-six years old, it was time a girl started thinking seriously about a husband, her mother had told her. They had just finished the midday meal, and Bay was expected to remain in the kitchen to help her sisters Nettie and

Tara wash dishes. But Bay knew that if she stayed, her mother would start talking about an Amish woman's responsibility to have a husband and a house full of children, and the conversation would go downhill from there.

Bay had been short with her mother, insisting she didn't have time to help with the dishes because she needed to get into town to buy more vegetable seeds and potting material for the family's gardening business. The greenhouse and shop had originally been her stepbrother Joshua's idea, but Bay had quickly discovered that she not only liked commercial gardening, but she had the head and the hands for it. Working with Joshua as an equal partner, she'd seen the business expand quickly in two years' time, and she'd done less and less housework. These days, Bay was more comfortable in the greenhouse or at the cash register than in the kitchen.

But then she had always been different than most Amish girls. When she was younger, she was the one that neighbors called a tomboy, and she'd always preferred outside chores. After her father passed away, she was the one who'd cared for their horses and cows, and tilled the garden. She'd carried her love of gardening with her when her family moved from upstate New York to Kent County, Delaware, four years ago.

Bay enjoyed getting her hands into the rich soil she made to pot seedlings and later to grow healthy vegetable and flower plants. It might have been sinful pride, but she secretly considered herself a match for any man in the county when it came to having a green thumb. It just seemed natural that she would work in the family's gardening business rather than in the house. She wasn't a very good cook, anyway, something her sisters teased her about. She could follow a written recipe well enough, but she didn't have the instincts her mother and sisters had. She barely knew the difference between white sugar and brown, and she never knew what spices to add to soups or stews.

The occasional raindrop began to turn into a pitter-patter on the wagon bed and on her head, covered only by a navy blue scarf. Bay looked skyward to see dark clouds coming in faster from the west. She should have taken one of the family buggies, but along with the seeds, she wanted to pick up several bales of peat moss and vermiculite, and she needed the wagon for that.

Glancing ahead, calculating how long it would take to get to the lawn and garden store in Seven Poplars, Bay wondered if she ought to turn around and head home. She was getting wet and she hadn't grabbed a raincoat. Instead, she was wearing one of her brothers' old denim jackets.

Ahead, she spotted a road that went off to the right, and she wondered where it came out. It seemed to lead north. Would it be a shortcut to Seven Poplars? she wondered. When she first started working in the gardening business, she and Joshua had spent lots of time wandering the local roads. Both of them enjoyed discovering new ways with less traffic to get around the county. But then he'd gotten married, and he no longer had as much time to spend with Bay as he used to.

On impulse, Bay urged Sassafras right, onto Persimmon Lane. As she turned, she noted a large drainage ditch to her right; the water was higher than usual due to heavy rain earlier in the week.

They weren't a quarter of a mile down the road when she heard a motor vehicle come up behind them and begin to pass. She caught a glimpse of the white pickup truck as it kicked up water off the road and sprayed the wagon.

Sassafras laid back her ears and snorted.

"Easy, girl," Bay murmured, gripping the leather reins tighter in her hands. Just as she spoke, the spray from the truck struck the mare and Sassafras let out a shrill whinny and reared in the traces.

"Whoa!" Bay cried as the wagon swayed and she fought to gain control of the startled horse.

The mare reared again and threw herself sideways, sending the wagon sliding off the road and down the ditch bank. Bay heard a loud snap and leaped off the wagon, managing to get free before she was caught in the tangle of thrashing hooves and the leather harness.

She landed hard on the bank on the far side and lay sprawled in the wet grass for a moment, the wind knocked out of her.

In his side-view mirror, David Jansen saw the horse rear, and he slammed on his brakes. Pulling over, and putting on his flashers, he threw his pickup into Park. He jumped out as the wagon slid off the road in what seemed like slow motion and tipped onto its side in the ditch. But where had the Amish woman in the green dress gone? She'd obviously been thrown from the wagon, but she wasn't lying on the road.

He was fast, but not fast enough to reach the overturned wagon before the young woman popped up and began making her way down the other side of the bank toward the thrashing animal. She must have been thrown clear, and appeared unhurt.

"Don't get near her!" David shouted above the sound of the flailing, whinnying horse.

But the woman didn't listen. As she scrambled to get to the animal, she spoke patiently to it, calling it Sassafras.

Heart in his throat, David ran toward her. "Wait!"

"I have to help her!" the woman cried. Now that David was closer, he could see that she was a woman close to his own age, with bright red hair. When he passed her on the road, he remembered she'd been wearing a wool scarf tied beneath her chin to cover her hair. It was gone now, and her hair tumbled wet down her back.

"Listen to me," he pleaded. He understood her need to help the animal, but he also knew how dangerous a frightened horse could be. He might be driving a pickup now, but he'd grown up Amish and had driven his share of horse-and-wagon teams.

Through the falling rain, David could see the mare trying to get to its feet, its eyes rolled back in its head in fear so that only the whites showed. It thrashed and neighed pitifully in the muck of the drainage ditch as it tried to find sure footing. "You can't do it that way!" he hollered.

"Help me, then," the woman cried, lifting her wet skirts as she reached the horse. "If I don't get her up—"

At that instant, his boot slipped on the wet grass and David fell hard, sliding down the bank into knee-deep water. "Just wait. I can help you," he shouted as he clumsily got to his feet, water filling his boots.

But she was paying him no mind as she waded through the cold water, brushing her hand along the horse's back and talking quietly to it. "Whoa, Sassafras. Easy, girl. Just give me a minute and I'll get you out of this."

The mare stilled, its head held at an awkward angle as the woman spoke soothingly and stroked the horse's haunch. David hoped that the old horse didn't have a broken leg. If a bone was shattered, it would be the end of the road for it. He knew from his farming days back in Wisconsin that sending an old horse off to some fancy veterinary hospital was beyond what an Amish family could afford. When a horse broke a leg, the animal was put down.

The woman reached the horse's head and stroked between its ears, using the same unruffled tone. "That a girl." Without looking at David, she said, "You have to help me get her out of the traces. I'll tell you what to do."

"You think that's wise?" Reaching the mare, he put out his hand to stroke her. "What if she's broken a leg?"

"I think she's all right." The woman began working a buckle on the harness. "I just have to—"

"I'll get the traces off. I've harnessed a few horses in my lifetime. You keep her calm." He moved slowly through the water, taking care to maintain his balance and not splash the horse. He didn't want to startle it. A frightened horse in this situation could kill a man trying to get free. Or a woman.

"My name's David. David Jansen. I live just up the road." He nodded in the direction of his farm, hoping his words would put the woman at ease. It had been his experience that some Amish women were uncomfortable around *English* men. Of course, he wasn't exactly an *Englisher*, but she didn't know that. "What's your name?"

She looked up at him and he was taken aback by how beautiful she was. She had a heart-shaped face with the most startling green eyes. And hair that was a striking, bright red. Being a redhead himself, he'd always had a thing for gingers.

The woman hesitated as if she wasn't sure she wanted to tell him her name. She returned her attention to her horse. "Bay," she responded. "Bay Stutzman. I live over in Hickory Grove. My stepfather, Benjamin, owns Miller's Harness Shop."

"Sorry, I don't know it." He bowed his head to get a better look at the harness. It was interesting, as he moved straps and tugged on buckles, how quickly the process came back to him.

In five minutes' time, the rain had eased and David had the harness off Sassafras. "You think you can lead her up and out or would you rather I did it?" he asked as he grabbed the horse's halter. "She might bolt when she comes to her feet."

"Just get back," Bay said, her tone short. "She won't hurt me, but she doesn't know you." She gave him a quick glance. "We wouldn't be in this ditch if you hadn't sped by and splashed water on her. That's what scared her." She shook her head. "You *Englishers*, you're always in such a hurry."

David wanted to defend himself; he hadn't been speeding. In fact, he'd taken his foot off the gas when he spotted them. It had just been an accident. And he wanted to tell her he wasn't an *Englisher*. That he'd grown up Amish and become Mennonite as a young man, but it didn't seem to be the right time. Instead, he moved up the bank, far enough to be out of the way, but close enough if Bay needed his help with the horse.

He watched the young Amish woman as she murmured into the mare's ear, then snapped a lead line onto the halter. The horse came easily to its feet in the ditch and stood patiently while Bay ran her hand down each of its legs.

"I think she's fine," Bay said without looking at David. "Back up. Here we come."

He moved over to where the wagon lay on its side in the ditch and watched as Bay led the horse up the slippery bank to the road. Once they were safely on the blacktop, he threw the harness on the wagon's seat and began looking over the vehicle. He was certain he could pull it out of the ditch with his truck, once it was righted…but it looked like there was damage to the rear wheel.

He looked up at Bay on the road now. It occurred to him that maybe he ought to get the reflective emergency triangles out of his pickup and set them up. But Persimmon Lane was never busy; sometimes only a dozen cars passed his place in a day. "Wheel's busted," he called up. "Not sure what else. We won't know until we get it out of the ditch."

He came up the bank, approaching Bay. "Do you have any way to call your husband? We could go up to my place so you can use the phone. Does he have a cell phone?" he asked, knowing that these days, some Amish men, particularly the younger ones, *did* have cell phones for work and emergencies.

"Don't you have a cellphone?" she asked, her tone indicating she was still annoyed with him.

"Accidentally left it home," he told her sheepishly. He kept stealing glances at her, telling himself he shouldn't, but he couldn't help it. Despite the annoyance in her voice, he had liked her at once. She was different than other Amish women he'd known. She was very sure of herself and he liked that.

She watched him as if trying to decide if he was trustworthy or not. Which was smart. David believed that most folks in the world were good people, but that didn't mean there weren't bad people out there, too.

The rain was beginning to fall again, and he adjusted his Clark Seed ball cap to keep his face dry. He cleared his throat. "Bay, I'm really sorry about this. I wasn't speeding.

I guess I caught the water from the trough made in the road by buggy wheels—"

"You're saying this is our fault?" Bay's green eyes widened with further irritation. "Everyone thinks that the Amish don't pay taxes, but we do. Our taxes pay for roads, you know. We have a right to the roads the same as you."

David looked away, pressing his lips together so he wouldn't smile. He liked the fire in her spirit. When he had control of his facial expression, he returned his gaze. "Anyhow, I'm sorry." He looked up at the sky that was darkening by the moment. "Do you have someone you can call from my house?"

She pursed her rosy lips in thought. "There's a phone in my stepfather's harness shop. I can call there and someone will come for Sassafras and me." She glanced at the wagon. "You think it will be safe here until morning? It looks like the weather is only going to get worse."

He nodded and glanced up as a streak of lightning zigzagged across the sky. "Let's put Sassafras in a stall and get her rubbed down. I imagine she'd appreciate a scoop of oats after what she's been through." He tilted his head in the direction of his farm. "I'm a quarter of a mile up the road, just around that corner." He put out his hand. "You want me to lead her?"

Bay frowned. "I can lead my own horse." She made a clicking sound between her teeth and started walking. The mare fell into step.

David hesitated, then began walking on the other side of the horse.

Bay looked at him over the mare's back. "Aren't you going to take your truck?" she asked as they went by his Ford parked on the side of the road.

"If you're walking in the rain, I'm walking in the rain." He stopped to open the driver's side door and grab the keys. Then he locked it and closed the door. "I'll come back for it."

Her mouth twitched almost to a smile. But not quite. "I can get her to your place on my own. I won't melt, you know."

He smiled at her. "Neither will I."

They fell into silence then, leaving the wagon and his truck behind. His wet boots were making a squeaking sound with every step he took. Anne had told him to take his rain jacket. Why hadn't he listened? But the walk wasn't far. He would dry just fine and so would his boots.

The horse's hooves made a rhythmic clip-clop as its metal-shod hooves hit the pavement, and David felt a wave of nostalgia wash over him. When he had left the Old Order Amish, it had been the right thing to do, but there were still times when he missed the slower pace of life. And the soothing sound of hoofbeats.

The rain began to come down harder and David and Bay both lowered their heads as they walked. At last they rounded the corner in the road, and he spotted his driveway ahead. "There's my place." He pointed.

"I appreciate your help." Bay's tone wasn't quite as cool now. "And I'm sorry about saying this was your fault. Sassafras can be skittish. If it's anyone's fault, it's mine. I chose to bring her out with a storm coming in." She lowered her head and kept walking. "I don't usually snap at strangers. I had a disagreement with my mother and—" She exhaled. "You don't want to hear about this."

Bay halted suddenly at the entrance to his driveway, and David heard the sounds of loose gravel, kicked up by Sassafras's hooves, skitter across the pavement. "Wait, this is your place?" She stared at the sign hanging from a post: Silver Maple Nurseries.

"It is."

She looked at him over the back of the horse. "You have a commercial nursery?"

"I do. I sell shrubs and trees. Mostly wholesale, but I've been playing with the idea of selling to the public."

"I have a greenhouse and garden shop," she said, her face lighting up.

And then she smiled, and David felt his insides flutter.

Chapter Two

Bay glanced again at the white-and-green sign that swung in the wind. How had she not known David had a commercial nursery only four miles from her? She'd thought she knew all of the local growers. She and Joshua had checked out the greenhouses and nurseries in their immediate area before starting their own business two years ago.

Thunder rumbled, followed by a crack of lightning that zigzagged across the sky, and she began walking again. David walked on the other side of Sassafras but didn't attempt to take the horse's halter. Most men, even her stepbrothers, would have insisted it was a man's job. The idea that David thought she was capable of leading her own horse in a thunderstorm intrigued her. Was it just because he was an *Englisher*, and it was their way? She didn't know many *English* men.

"Have you been in Kent County long?" she asked, the sound of Sassafras's horseshoes clanging on his paved driveway.

"Nope." David flipped up the collar of his corduroy coat that was wet with rain. "I moved here from Wisconsin just after Christmas. Had a nursery business there, too."

She nodded, trying to ignore how cold she was all of a sudden. She supposed the shock of the accident and her concern for the safety of the mare had kept her from feeling the temperature dropping, but now that she no longer had adrenaline rushing through her body, she was shivering. "We've got good soil in the area." Her gaze flicked to his as she wondered how old he was. Older than her, for sure. Maybe thirty? *And handsome*.

But also an *Englisher*, she reminded herself.

And more likely than not, he was married.

She was surprised at her thoughts. She never considered men that way. More fuel for her mother's concern she would end up an old maid.

She glanced at David. He had a strong jaw and was clean-shaven. He was a redhead with blue eyes. "I imagine you had good soil back in Wisconsin, too, but we have a milder climate here. And a longer growing season." She chuckled. "My family moved here from upstate New York a few years ago. We used to shovel a lot of snow."

David grinned, nodding. "Definitely a milder climate here. And I have to say, I didn't miss having to shovel my way to the barn in January and February."

The rain began to fall harder, and Bay walked faster. Stealing another glance at David over the mare's back, she reached out and stroked the horse's flank. "Good girl. Almost there. You'll be inside, warm and safe, soon enough. Not a great day to be out," she directed toward David. "I was headed to the new feedstore over in Seven Poplars—Faulkner's. You know it?"

He met her gaze, and she felt the strangest sensation, something like a tickle at the nape of her neck. It wasn't unpleasant, but it was definitely unfamiliar.

"I do know Faulkner's. I like them as well as Clark's." He slid his hands into his coat pockets; he looked as cold as she felt. "Been there a couple of times for vermiculite. They have good bulk prices."

"I was going for vermiculite," she responded, appreciating their shared interest. "And bales of peat. That's why I took the wagon instead of the buggy." She shook her head. "Guess I should have checked the weather forecast."

"Day like this," David said, "I'd think you'd have sent your husband."

Bay laughed aloud. Why, she wasn't sure. Maybe because the argument that had led to her leaving the house so imprudently had been about the very fact that she *didn't* have a husband. Or maybe because there was a strange, nervous excitement rippling through her, making her feel off-kilter.

He frowned, his dark red brows moving closer together. "I say something funny?"

She shook her head, surprising herself with a giggle more suitable to one of her younger sisters than herself. "*Ne*, I'm not laughing at you. I'm laughing at myself." Her gaze strayed to the trees that lined the driveway.

The row nearest to the driveway looked like dogwoods. White dogwood, probably. Her favorite. They grew well in the area and had the most gorgeous white flowers. And there was a second line of trees that were easy to identify because they were about to burst into bloom. Cherry trees, also a favorite of hers.

David waited, watching her over Sassafras's back, a hint of a smile on his face.

She glanced his way, then shifted her gaze to look forward again, wondering what her mother would think if she knew she was alone with a male stranger. It wasn't the Amish way. And to make matters worse, she'd somehow lost her headscarf when the wagon went into the ditch. An Amish woman was never supposed to be without a head covering except in the presence of her husband. Her mother wouldn't be pleased about that, for sure. She wished she'd looked for it back at the scene of the accident, but she'd been more worried about Sassafras's safety than proper attire.

"My mother and I argued today," Bay heard herself say. "About me still being single with no prospects. I left the house with the excuse of going for supplies, but I really just wanted to get away from her."

"I'm sorry to hear that. I know from experience that can be hard, being an adult, living with your parents."

"*Ya*, yes," Bay corrected, adjusting her speech for the *Englisher* the way she did when she waited on them in her garden shop. "That's for sure. My twin sister got married and ever since, my mother has been pushing me to 'find a good Amish man to make me his wife,'" she said, using her mother's words. "It seems like that's all she wants to talk about."

He was quiet for a moment and then asked, "You don't want to marry?" She could detect no judgment in his tone, just curiosity.

"No, not…well, I don't know. Definitely not yet." She exhaled. "It's not that I'm too old. That's my mother's fear, I think, that no one will marry me, so she wants me to start looking. She thinks I'm too independent to suit most Amish men. *Mam* is afraid I'll be an old maid like her aunt Dorcas, who lived with her family when she was growing up."

"She thinks no one would want to marry you?" David chuckled. "I hardly think that's a concern."

She felt herself blush. *Was he complimenting her?* "I think she's worried that my greenhouse business will be off-putting to Amish men, and I don't want to give it up. But it's not really our way. Women working."

He frowned, wiping the rain from his forehead. "But plenty of Amish women work. I see them in Byler's and at Fifer's Orchard, too."

"*Ya*, but they're mostly unmarried women or women whose children are grown. And that's working at a counter. Those women aren't running their own businesses. They're

still home in the mornings to make breakfast and then back by late afternoon to make
supper. And clean. And do wash. And make
bread, and…and all the things we do in a
day."

"I would think your mother would be proud
of you, owning your own business."

"Oh, it's not just mine. I own it with my
brother."

"Still, even owning *half* a business, I'd think
your mother would be pleased that you're so
capable."

She laughed. "I think she'd like me to be a
little more capable in the house. In the kitchen,
in particular."

"Not much of a cook?" he asked, the
amusement in his tone again.

"I can follow a recipe well enough, but I get
distracted and put in too much baking pow-
der or not enough." She shrugged. "Just not
all that interested in cooking, I guess."

He nodded thoughtfully. "And your father?
What does he think of you being a business-
woman?"

"My father passed years ago. Benjamin is
my mother's second husband. I'm not sure
what he thinks about me working. Probably
whatever my mother thinks—just to keep her
happy." She flashed him a smile. "I didn't in-

tend to get into the gardening business. It just sort of happened. The greenhouse and shop were my stepbrother Joshua's dream, but then we realized I had a knack for it, and somehow, I ended up part owner."

"Right, I guess that is unusual. An Amish woman owning a business, running it."

"It is, especially since we're Old Order. I mean, I know women who sell poultry or eggs, or make quilts to sell so they have their own pin money, but— You know what pin money is?" she asked.

"I do. It's a woman's personal money. My mother embroidered Bible verses for her pin money. She framed them herself and sold them in a little country store where I grew up, near Madison."

She was impressed that he knew the term. And was curious about his upbringing. She wanted to ask him to tell her more about growing up in Wisconsin, but it didn't seem appropriate. It was likely she'd never see this man again. She didn't even know why she wanted to know those things.

Ahead, the lane opened up in front of them and a barnyard appeared. It looked remarkably like every Amish barnyard in Kent County: a big, gambrel-roofed barn and several outbuildings, all well cared for. And there was a white, two-story farmhouse with a big front porch. There were goats in a small pasture on one side of the drive and three horses in a larger one on the other side. In the distance, she heard the bleat of goats and the cluck-clucking of chickens. There was even a shiny, new windmill. The only real difference between her place and David's was the wires over their heads that stretched from the road to the house and some of the buildings, carrying electricity. And the three huge greenhouses she saw in the distance in a field on the back of the property.

David met her gaze. "I'm sorry about the disagreement with your mother."

"Thank you." Bay gave him a quick smile. "It'll be fine. She only wants what's best for me. And what's best for our community. It's important that we keep up our Amish traditions."

"And going against that can be very hard," he agreed. "I know. I've been there."

She glanced at him, curious as to how he knew about going up against traditions, when thunder clapped loudly overhead. The boom was followed immediately by another streak of lightning in the sky. And then the rain fell harder.

"Come on, let's get her in the barn and

rubbed down," David said, heading in the direction of the main barn.

Twenty minutes later, Sassafras was tucked in a stall of David's immaculately kept barn, a scoop of oats in a trough in front of her. The rain had let up a bit, and Bay and David dashed across the barnyard toward his back porch. As they hurried up the steps, the door swung open and a pretty woman about Bay's age, wearing a calf-length dress similar to hers and a lace head covering, stepped out onto the porch.

She had to be his wife.

And she was Mennonite. She knew a few Mennonite women and they all wore a small bit of lace on the back of their head rather than a full prayer *kapp* like Bay and her family wore.

They were Mennonite, she realized. David was Mennonite. She should have guessed. A man driving a white pickup truck, living on a farm that looked like an Amish farm, and just how he carried himself. He was polite and friendly in a wholesome way.

"David?" the young woman said, wiping her hands on a pale blue full apron tied over her protruding belly. "I didn't hear the truck come up the lane. Is everything all right?"

"Fine. Anne, this is Bay. She lives down

the road. She had a little run-in with a ditch in her wagon. We put her horse up in the barn until someone can come for them. She needs to use the phone."

A little boy of maybe three years old peered out from behind David's wife. David's son, obviously. When Bay made eye contact with the boy, he hid behind his mother again.

"Oh my, are you all right?" Anne moved aside, almost stepping on the little boy. "Matty, get inside," she told him, though not unkindly. "You've got bare feet. You'll catch a chill."

The little boy darted back into the house.

"Come in, please," David's wife said. "You're soaked through." She stepped aside, waving Bay past her. "Why did you walk home, David? You should have brought her in the truck. She's soaked. The both of you are."

"It's not his fault," Bay said, stepping into a large mudroom that looked similar to her mother's. A clothes dryer was running, and the room smelled of wet shoes, fabric softener and gingerbread. She saw a basket on the floor with a mother cat inside, nursing several black-and-white kittens. "I had to walk my mare here," she told Anne. "He didn't want me walking alone."

Anne followed Bay into the laundry room.

"You're brave to walk a horse in this storm. Please, come into the kitchen and I'll get you something hot to drink. Would you like tea or coffee?"

Bay stepped out of her soaking wet black sneakers, wondering why she hadn't had the sense to put on her rubber boots when she left the house. Next, she peeled off her coat, which Anne took from her and hung on the wall hook. "I don't want to trouble you."

"No trouble at all. The kettle's already on."

"Tea would be nice, then," Bay said.

"Tea it is." Anne turned to David. "Don't you even think about wearing those boots in the house. I just mopped the kitchen."

He lowered his head sheepishly, then winked at Bay and sat down on a bench to unlace his work boots.

Bay was so surprised by his wink that she froze for a moment. What kind of man would wink at another woman right in front of his wife?

"Please come in," Anne said again, walking into the kitchen. If she had seen David wink at Bay, she gave no indication. "I'll have that tea ready in just a minute. Tea, David?"

"Coffee," he called from the bench where he was still wrestling with his wet boots.

"You've had enough coffee for today."

Anne flashed Bay a smile as she walked toward a kitchen counter where an electric teakettle was beginning to whistle. "He'll be up half the night if he drinks anymore coffee." Then to David she called, "Tea or hot chocolate?"

The country kitchen was almost as big as the one at home, with a big, six-burner gas stove with two ovens. The floors were polished hardwood, the walls white, the countertops some sort of shiny stone, and the cabinets were all painted a cheery yellow. Gingham white-and-yellow curtains were pulled back from the windows, which looked to have been recently cleaned.

"Hot chocolate sounds good," David hollered from the laundry room. "With *mashmallows*, right, Matty?" He mispronounced the word, obviously for the benefit of the boy who was now under the table. "We like *mashmallows*."

The boy said nothing.

"Matty, come out from under there," Anne ordered. When he made no attempt to move, she said, "Come out and you can have hot chocolate with Uncle David. With *mashmallows*."

David was Matty's uncle?

Which meant Anne was his sister, not his

wife. Bay glanced at David, now standing in the doorway. *If Anne wasn't his wife, where was his wife?*

Or maybe he was single.

The moment the thought went through her head, she tamped it down. It was so unlike her to be concerned whether a man was married or not. What did she care? She wasn't looking for a husband. And certainly not one outside her faith. Bay only knew one person who had left the Amish community to become Mennonite and that was Hannah Hartman's daughter Leah. Leah had married a Mennonite and gone to South America with him to do mission work.

"I'm going to run upstairs and change," David said, his wet socks leaving spots on the wood floor as he crossed the kitchen. "I'll be right back, Bay. The phone's there on the wall." He pointed to a dial wall phone. "Anne, can you find Bay a blanket or something?"

Anne poured the hot water into a white teapot painted with blue and yellow flowers. When the sound of David's footsteps echoed on the stairs, she turned to Bay. "Go ahead and call home. I imagine your family must be worried about you."

Bay dialed the phone number to the harness shop and one of the girls who worked at the front counter answered. She told Emily what had happened, assuring her that she and the horse were fine when the girl got flustered. Then she gave her the directions to David's place and hoped for the best. Emily wasn't always the best at relaying phone messages, because she never seemed to get them right. She either missed a digit of a number or forgot to write down the reason for the call in the first place.

"Someone's coming for me," Bay told Anne when she hung up.

"Good. In the meantime, can I get you some dry clothes?" Anne asked.

Bay touched her wet hair and felt her cheeks grow warm with embarrassment. She didn't know who would come for her and the mare, but she doubted any of the men in her family would appreciate her being bareheaded. "I lost my headscarf when I had the accident. My dress will dry, but if you have a scarf I can borrow, I'd appreciate it." Out of the corner of her eye, she saw Matty peeking out from under the round table, which was covered with a tablecloth with buttercups embroidered on it. "We don't let our hair go uncovered. But you probably know that."

Anne smiled at her as she carried the teapot to the table. "Ah. So, David told you that we grew up Amish?"

That surprised Bay, but then she realized it shouldn't have. Many Mennonite families had once been Amish. "*Ne*...no. He didn't."

Anne shook her head as she went into the laundry room and came back carrying a dark blue wool headscarf that looked similar to the one Bay had lost. In her other hand, Anne had a pair of blue socks. "At least put on some dry socks," she told Bay, offering both items. "You'll feel warmer."

Bay considered saying *no, thank you*, but the practicality of Anne's offer overrode any sense of awkwardness she felt. She was always so sensible, always making good choices. Taking the wagon out when bad weather was coming in was so out of character for her. She didn't know what had gotten into her. "Thank you," she murmured, accepting the items.

"Matty, come out from under there," Anne ordered, pointing her finger. "This is our new friend, Bay. Can you say hello?"

The little boy peeked out from under the tablecloth and then slowly pushed out one of the chairs.

"Is this for me?" Bay asked him.

Matty nodded slowly, watching her with big brown eyes.

"Thank you," Bay told him as she sat down to change her socks.

"It's not you," Anne said, carrying two mugs to the table. "Matty's shy. Has been for some months now." Her eyes started to tear up and she turned away. "Milk and sugar for your tea, Bay?"

"Just sugar." Wondering what had made Anne sad, Bay remade her bun and covered her wet hair with the scarf, tying it at the nape of her neck.

Anne wrinkled her nose. "You sound just like me. I don't care for milk. I know. A girl who grew up Amish on a dairy farm who doesn't drink milk." She tilted her head, looking under the table. "Matthew, if you want cookies with that hot chocolate, you'd best run and wash your hands. I saw you playing with those kittens when I turned my back. We have new kittens," she explained, returning her attention to Bay. "A stray female someone dropped off at the end of the lane. David is such a softy. He brought her inside and made a nice bed for her in the laundry room and two days later, we had six cats instead of one."

The ladder-back chair opposite the one Bay

was seated at scraped the floor, and Matty darted out from under the table and ran out of the kitchen.

As Bay was putting the dry navy knee socks on, Anne brought over a plate of home-made gingerbread cookies. "I hope you'll excuse my son's behavior. He's very wary around strangers and doesn't really talk anymore. Not since his father passed."

"I'm so sorry," Bay breathed, glancing at Anne's round abdomen. "And you—" She cut herself off before she said *expecting*. Among the Amish, one didn't bring up pregnancy with strangers. She didn't know if it was the same with Mennonite women.

"Thank you." Anne sighed and stroked her belly. "It's been bittersweet. I lost my husband, Matthew, to a car accident last fall, but God saw fit to bless us with another child all the same."

Bay balled up her wet socks and carried them to her shoes in the mudroom. When she returned to the kitchen, Anne was spooning cocoa mix from a big blue tub into two mugs. "I can't imagine how hard it's been for you," she said quietly. "You moved here from Wisconsin, too?"

"When Matthew and I married. He has a brother who lives in Greenwood. We were renting an apartment in Dover, looking for the right property. Matthew had always wanted a greenhouse business and when this place came up for sale, we bought it. He had big plans for this spring." She pressed her lips together, going quiet for a moment. "But it wasn't meant to be." She flashed a smile at Bay. "I was trying to decide if I was going to have to sell and move back to Wisconsin." She leaned against the counter. "I knew I'd need help when the little one arrived, but I didn't want to leave our church. Kent County had just begun to feel like home, and I didn't want to leave my friends or my midwife. Then David offered to sell his place and come here to live with us and take over the business and…" Tears filled her eyes. "I'm sorry." She lifted the hem of her apron and patted her eyes. "You don't want to hear all of this. I don't know how I started down this path." She sniffed. "Hormones, I guess."

Bay stood in the middle of the kitchen for a moment, not sure what to do. Her impulse was to give Anne a hug. Anne just looked like she needed it. It occurred to Bay as she moved toward her that Anne might not want a hug from a wet stranger, but when she opened her arms, Anne looked relieved.

"I'm sorry I'm wet," Bay murmured.

Anne put her arms around Bay. "Thank you," she whispered.

The two stood, hugging for a moment, and then Anne took a step back, pulling a hankie from her apron pocket to wipe her nose. "Matty," she called. "Your hot chocolate is ready. I'm just trying to figure out if you want marshmallows or not." She flashed Bay a mischievous smile. "He hears just fine, just not interested in talking again yet. His pediatrician said to give him time. Losing a father at Matty's age is traumatic. We were hoping that when David moved in, Matty might find his voice, but so far..." She sighed, then looked up at Bay. "All in God's time, right?" She picked up the two mugs of hot chocolate she'd made and carried them to the table. "Enough of this talk. Tell me about yourself, Bay. Do you have children? Please have your tea before it gets too cool." Anne motioned to the table.

Bay slipped back into her chair, thinking how much she liked Anne. She was so positive for a woman who had been through so much. And she seemed like she'd be fun. There was a sparkle in her eyes that made Bay smile. "No children. No husband."

Anne had just turned away from the table but turned back, her calf-length skirt swishing. "Oooh, single? And no beau?" she asked, narrowing her gaze coyly.

Bay laughed and took a sip of tea. "Funny you should say that. The fact that I have no husband or beau is how I ended up in the ditch." She tipped her head to one side. "In a roundabout way."

Just then, Bay heard the sound of David's footsteps as he came down the stairs. A moment later, he walked back into the kitchen with Matty trailing.

"Did you know Bay is single?" Anne asked her brother as he took the chair opposite Bay at the head of the table. Matty climbed into the chair to his uncle's left.

David smiled from across the table at Bay and, against her will, she felt a little flutter in her chest.

"David's single, too," Anne announced, sliding into the chair on the other side of her brother as she looked from him to Bay and back at him again.

Any other man would have been embarrassed, but David just threw his head back and laughed, and Bay was almost glad she'd driven into the thunderstorm.

Chapter Three

"'The end,'" David read softly. Closing the book, he looked down at his nephew in bed, his little hands tucked beneath his head as if praying as he slept. The sight of the boy sleeping so soundly brought a lump of emotion to his throat. He wondered what it would be like to have his own son or daughter. Because if this feeling of joy was what children brought into his life, maybe it was time he thought about looking for a wife. He always knew he would marry someday, but he'd never been in a hurry to take that next step. Why was he thinking about it tonight?

He gazed at Matty with a smile. The boy had the same red hair that David and his sister had. Would his own child be a redhead? The three-year-old looked so much like Anne that Matty's father, Matthew, had joked that their child was a Jansen through and through. But David saw Matthew in the boy's brown eyes, in his facial expressions and in his kindness to all creatures from the tiniest insect to their massive Clydesdale horse.

David set the Laura Ingalls Wilder picture book on the nightstand, adding it to a whole stack of them that he and Anne had found at a local flea market. One of Anne's friends from her Mennonite church had brought the first one to Matty after his father died, and the boy had clung to it for days. He had David and Anne read them over and over again. When David found another one of the books, he'd brought it home and he and Anne had laughed that he had bought it for his own sanity. He didn't know how many times more he could read *Little House in the Big Woods* to Matty. Now there was a whole stack of them to read to the boy. In fact, they owned two copies of a couple of books because Matty carried them around the house, out into the barnyard, the fields and the greenhouses, and the original copies had gotten too tattered to read.

David swept the hair off Matty's forehead and slid back in his chair, his thoughts drifting from the boy to his day. More specifically, to Bay Stutzman.

A smile lifted the corners of his mouth.

"A good thing I saw the accident in the rear-view mirror, wasn't it?" he said softly to his nephew. The boy hadn't spoken since he learned of his father's death six months ago, but David made a point of talking to him, anyway. Even when he was asleep. "I feel terrible enough as it is for unintentionally causing Bay's accident, but I'm afraid to think what might have happened if I hadn't been there."

He smirked. "Who am I kidding, Matty? She'd have been just fine. She'd have gotten her mare out of the traces. Probably walked all the way home in that thunderstorm."

He couldn't stop smiling. "She was nice, don't you think? Spirited." He leaned forward and tucked the handmade log cabin quilt around the boy. "And pretty."

David continued, keeping his voice low. "You thought she was pretty, didn't you? I saw you looking at her from under the table. You liked her, too." He nodded thoughtfully. "You're a good judge of character, little man. At least for a three-year-old," he added.

He shifted his gaze to the curtained window on the far wall. "There was just something about Bay that made me feel…good. You know, happy. In here." He tapped his chest over his heart. Then he exhaled. "I know. I know what you're thinking. She's Old Order Amish. She would never be interested in a man like me. When she marries, it will be to a man in the Old Order church. The two of us? It can't happen." He closed his eyes. "But Matty," he whispered. "I wish it could. A woman so smart and beautiful and independent. And she loves plants like me. She—"

The bedroom door that David had left half-open creaked, and he turned around in the chair.

"Matty, what are you doing still—" Anne stepped into the room and glanced at her son, a look of surprise on her face. "Oh, he's sound asleep."

Slightly embarrassed to have been caught talking to a sleeping child, David rose from the chair and moved it to its place on the far side of the nightstand. "He is. He was out by the time we got to Pa and the bee tree."

She frowned, looking tired. "Then who were you talking to?" she asked.

He shrugged. "Myself, I guess," he answered sheepishly. Something he had been doing frequently since his arrival in Delaware. He hadn't made any friends yet and he missed having friends or family to talk with. Sure, he and Anne talked. A lot. But there were some matters, like his worries concerning her health, that he couldn't talk to her about. Also topics like pretty, single women, too.

He followed Anne out of the bedroom, sliding the dimmer light down until the lamp on the nightstand beside Matty's bed barely glowed. Since his father's death, Matty had not only stopped talking, but he had become afraid of the dark. In the first days after his father's passing, he hadn't been able to sleep unless it was in his mother's bed. Only after David had moved in had Matty been convinced to return to his own room.

"I thought you'd gone to sleep," David said, redirecting the conversation. "You said you were going to bed. You know what the midwife said. You can't be on your feet all day without resting. Not with the hours you keep. At the very least, you need to be getting to bed earlier."

Standing in the hall, she pulled off her apron that was dusty with flour, likely from the buttermilk biscuits she had made to go with the ham and scalloped potatoes and roasted Brussel sprouts they'd had for supper. "I'm going. I just have to get the dried beans soaking to make a soup with that ham bone tomorrow."

"I'll do it."

"David, you already do so much. I hate to—"

"What? You think I can't dump a bag of beans into some water?"

"And add salt, or they won't taste right," she added.

"I've got it, Anne. So…" He opened his arms wide. "Go on, get to bed."

"I'm going. Stop fussing over me," she said, as she headed down the hall.

David was turning to go in the opposite direction when Anne turned back to him.

"I liked her. Bay," she said. "And I think you did, too," she added, a hint of playfulness in her voice.

He didn't look back as he strode toward the staircase landing. "She was nice enough," he answered, trying to keep his tone neutral.

"She's very pretty," Anne called after him. "You should ask her out."

He stopped, his hand on the staircase rail. "Anne, she's Amish. And we no longer are. Bay and I…that would be impossible."

She gave a little laugh. "That's where you're mistaken, Davy," she responded, using his childhood nickname, one she knew he disliked. "Anything is possible with God."

David didn't answer, but he lay in bed

awake for a very long time that night, thinking about Bay, and imagining what it would like to love and be loved by a woman like her.

That night, Bay lay awake in bed into the wee hours of the morning, listening to the sounds of her sisters Nettie and Tara sleeping. She couldn't sleep because her thoughts were all a jumble in her mind. She kept rehashing the conversations she'd had with her mother and with David.

That evening, after returning from David's with her brothers, Bay had waited until after supper to have a private conversation with her mother. Something that wasn't easy in their household. She'd found her *mam* in the pantry after the kitchen was clean and her family had scattered to finish their tasks of the day before gathering in the parlor for evening prayers. Her mother, Rosemary, was adding flour to the sourdough starter she'd been keeping since she was a new bride nearly thirty years ago. She had brought her starter from her first marriage to Bay's father, to her second marriage to Benjamin Miller. While Bay wasn't much of a baker, it was a comforting continuation in a world that seemed to be changing quickly, a world where she no longer knew exactly where she belonged.

Bay's father and Benjamin had been the best of friends. It only seemed right that Benjamin, also widowed, would eventually come calling on Bay's mother. Both had a houseful of children and a farm to care for on their own. It had been logical to the Amish way of thinking that the two should join their two households. What had been surprising was that they had fallen in love. It had been a daring move, trying to meld two families with adult or nearly adult children together, but they had made it work.

Bay rolled onto her back in her bed.

As she had stood in the doorway of the pantry that evening, she'd wondered if the reason she was so opposed to marriage was that she was afraid. Her mother had found love not once but twice in her lifetime. Bay's sisters Lovey and Ginger and her stepbrothers Joshua, Ethan and Levi had all married for love. Benjamin's only daughter, Mary, had, as well. But what if no one ever fell in love with Bay? What if her liberated ways made her unlovable? She knew that some women in their community married for reasons other than romantic love, but Bay wanted to love and be loved and if that weren't possible, she would rather remain single for the rest of her days.

Her mother had taken a proofing jar from

a shelf and removed the flat, glass lid. She was a pretty woman still, even on the downside of her forties, as she liked to say. She had a comely face with a clear complexion and no visible wrinkles. Her eyes were nearly the same color as Bay's. She wore her brown hair in a bun at the nape of her neck, a pristine white prayer *kapp* on her head, and she was nearly as slim as Bay. For years she had been a little plump, but after the birth of Bay's two little brothers after they moved to Delaware, she had slimmed down to the body of a much younger woman. It was chasing after the boys that had brought down her weight, she insisted. Whether that was true or not, Bay thought she looked far younger than a woman nearing fifty.

"There you are," Bay had said softly. "I was looking for you."

"And here I am," her mother had replied. She hadn't looked at her, but there had been no crossness in her tone.

Bay had watched her pour off part of the starter so she could add fresh flour to keep the *mother*—the pre-fermented dough—alive. "I wanted to—" She had sighed. Apologizing had never been easy for her. It wasn't that she never regretted things she said and did, only that she found it trying to find the words to say so. "I'm sorry about our argument earlier today."

With the sourdough *mother* divided, Bay's *mam* had measured out flour from a five-gallon plastic tub. "I wasn't aware we argued, *Dochter*." She'd glanced at Bay in the doorway.

Bay had hung her head. "It felt like we did." She'd looked up. "And it felt like you were criticizing me for who I am."

Her *mam* had sighed and wiped her hands on her apron, turning to her. "I'm sorry if it sounded that way." Green eyes had met green eyes. "I didn't mean to criticize you. I love your free spirit, Bay. We all do. It's only that Benjamin and I worry about you. About your future. This time in your life is so crucial, and I don't want to see you make mistakes that could affect the rest of your life. This is when you should be going to singings and frolics and taking buggy rides with eligible young men." She had rested a hand, dusty with flour, on her hip. "Do you want to spend the rest of your life in your mother's home, never having one of your own? Your own family?"

"You and Benjamin *are* my family. My sisters and brothers are my family."

Her *mam* had put the lid back on the flour

container. She had been wearing a peach-colored dress and even in the dusky light of the pantry, it made her skin look rosy and fresh. "You know what I mean." She'd given Bay an all-knowing eye.

"*Ya*, that you're afraid I'll never marry. That I'll be an old maid." Bay had studied her slippers, trying not to grow impatient with her mother the way she had earlier in the day. "Would that really be such a terrible thing, I mean, if I didn't marry," Bay had asked. "I'd be around to take care of you and Benjamin. We care for our own when they get old. You say that all the time."

Her mother had laughed. "Old, are we? Tell those little brothers of yours that." In the direction of the toddlers' bedroom, she had pointed upward to where they were, hopefully sound asleep. "Maybe they'll stop running me ragged."

Bay had looked away, a lump rising in her throat. She admired her mother. She loved her deeply, but she didn't feel like her mother really listened to her. "You always take what I'm saying in the wrong way. I didn't say you were old. But one day you will get old, *Mam*." She had let out a frustrated sigh. "Not all women marry, you know. Some stay home and care for their parents."

"Hmm," her mother had intoned. "And here Benjamin and I were looking forward to, someday, many years in the future, having some time to ourselves. The way we had at the beginning of our first marriages—before we had children."

Bay hadn't been sure how to respond, so she'd said nothing.

Her mother had stared at her for what seemed like a long time before she had spoken again. "I just want you to be happy, Bay. I want you to live a long, happy life of faith and good deeds."

"And I can't have faith in God and do good without a husband wrapped around my neck?" The moment the words had come out of Bay's mouth, she had regretted them. She had gone to apologize, not start another quarrel.

Her mother hadn't taken her words poorly, though, in fact, she had chuckled. "When you say it that way, it doesn't have a lot of appeal, does it?"

Bay hadn't been able to resist a little smile as she had lifted her gaze to her mother again. "I'm not saying I will never marry. I'm only saying that…" She had exhaled, her thoughts darting back to her accident earlier in the day. To David. She had pushed them aside.

"I haven't met anyone I like well enough even to consider marriage. You wouldn't want me to marry someone I didn't want to live the rest of my life with, would you? You want me to find someone I'm suited to."

Her mother had narrowed her gaze. "It seems to me that a certain young woman told me today in my kitchen that she was never, *ever* going to marry and that I couldn't make her do it." She had gestured. "As if I was going to drag you to your wedding by your apron strings."

Bay had felt her cheeks grow warm. "I was upset, *Mam*. You know how I can be. I say things sometimes that I don't mean."

"Oh, *Dochter*." Her had mother crossed the short distance between them and put her arms around Bay. "I'm so glad that you weren't hurt today. I feel as if it were my fault, you taking off the way you did with a thunderstorm coming in."

Bay had returned the hug, breathing in the scent of her mother, a mixture of flour, vanilla and love that she knew would always be present. "It wasn't your fault. I'm a hothead. Or becoming one," she had admitted, stepping back. "And I'm fine. The mare's fine."

"And the wagon?"

"Not quite as fine. Jacob said he and Jesse

would go in the morning and try to pull it out of the ditch. It was raining too hard by the time they arrived to get Sassafras and me, and he wanted to get us home."

"That was kind of those folks to help you."

"*Ya*, Anne was so nice." Bay had pressed her lips together, not sure why she'd mentioned Anne's name and not David's. "She gave me socks to wear because my feet had gotten wet." She left out the bit about the scarf, thinking there was no need for her mother to know that David had seen her bareheaded.

Her mother had returned to the counter to finish the sourdough starter. "I plan to make cinnamon rolls in the morning." She had begun to stir the flour into the pre-fermented dough. "You said Anne's Mennonite? I bet the family would appreciate homemade cinnamon rolls. You should take them some."

"I'm sure they would. I was thinking I would go with the boys to get the wagon and…return Anne's socks." As she spoke, Bay realized she really wanted to go back to David's place. To thank him and Anne. In fact, her need to go almost felt desperate. "I could take the rolls, too."

"I think that would be lovely."

Their conversation had ended with Bay's

mother giving her a peck on the cheek as she left the pantry. It was decided. Bay would go back to Anne and David's home with the cinnamon rolls to say thank-you.

Bay rolled over in her bed, pulling the patchwork quilt, which her mother had made her, to her chin. That was what was keeping her awake now. Thinking about David. She kept going over every word he'd said, every gesture he had made. His wink. What had that been all about? No one had ever winked at her before. Which had her intrigued.

She closed her eyes, wondering if it would be wrong to pray to God that David would be there again in the morning.

The following day, one that had turned out to be sunny and reasonably warm, Bay found herself standing beside her stepbrother Jacob and brother Jesse, staring at the drainage ditch on Persimmon Lane. David's road. Where there was no wagon.

"I don't understand," she worried aloud. "I'm sure this is the place." She pointed. "Look, you can see the ruts the wheels made as I slid into the ditch." She'd been going over and over in her mind what she was going to say to David when she took the cinnamon rolls to him. Them, she corrected. She had planned out everything she was going to say and how she was going to say it. She even had a contingency plan for what to do if he winked at her again. She was going to call him on it—ask if he'd winked at her or if he'd only had dust in his eye. He'd likely laugh. She liked the idea of making him laugh because she had loved the sound of it. She had the whole morning planned out. What she hadn't planned on was the wagon not being there where they had left it the night before.

Jacob glanced around, taking in the field beyond the drainage ditch and the woods behind them, across the road. "I know this is the place. It was here last night when we went by."

Jesse tugged at the brim of his straw hat, imitating Jacob as he looked one way down the road then the other. While he had grown taller over the winter, her little brother was still small for his age. Wiry. As his face matured, he reminded her more and more of their father. "This is the place, all right. You think someone stole it?" he asked, seeming excited by the idea.

Jacob shrugged. "I guess it's possible, but who? This road isn't well-traveled. And what would an *Englisher* do with an old horse-drawn wagon with a broken wheel? How would they get it down the road?"

Bay stared at the ditch, hands on her hips. "I bet I know where it is."

Five minutes later, Bay stood at David's back door, the disposable pan of cinnamon rolls in her hands. As she waited for someone to answer the door, she glanced over her shoulder. Jacob and Jesse were waiting in the wagon they had borrowed that morning. With the tools they had piled in the back, they were hoping to repair their wagon and tow it home.

Was no one home? Bay knocked again and looked into the barnyard, where there was no sign of their wagon. She had thought David had brought it back to his place to keep it safe until they came. Now it was looking more as if Jesse had been right. Maybe someone had stolen it.

A sound on the other side of the door caught Bay's attention. She saw the doorknob turn and looked up, hoping it would be David. So she could thank him properly. And tell him about the stolen wagon, she guessed.

But when the door opened, no one was there.

Actually, someone was.

When she looked downward, she saw Anne's little boy. "Matty. Hi, there, remember me from yesterday? I'm Bay." She crouched down to look at him eye to eye.

"I brought something delicious for you and your *mam* and D—your uncle." He was an adorable little boy with red hair the same shade as David and Anne's, but darker than her own. She'd always adored red-haired children, maybe because she knew what it was like to grow up a redhead. People made all kinds of assumptions about redheads: they had terrible tempers, were badly behaved and had minds of their own. Well…maybe the last one was true. Anyway, she knew what it was like to be teased in the schoolyard and have your hair pulled while kids called you carrottop.

"Do you like cinnamon rolls?" She showed him the container. "With orange frosting," she enticed.

Matty nodded, his eyes widening with approval.

"Then I think you should have one, but only if your mother says it's okay. Is your mama here?"

"I'm here!" called Anne from inside. "Come on in, Bay."

Bay walked into the laundry room and pulled the back door closed behind her. From the doorway between the laundry room and the kitchen, she spotted Anne standing on the fourth rung of a stepladder.

"We saw you pull up in the driveway," Anne said. "It's just that I—"

"Can I get that for you?" Bay rushed to the kitchen table to set down the rolls.

Anne was trying to lower a stack of colorful ceramic baking dishes, one nested inside the other. The problem was that it appeared they were heavy, and she was having a problem keeping herself balanced on the top of the stepstool.

"No...actually, yes," Anne said with a laugh, half born of frustration, half of relief. "David said I shouldn't put these up here, that it's too high for me." Leaving the dishes on the top of the kitchen cabinet, she slowly came down the stepstool, using the countertop to keep her balance. "But who likes to tell a man when they're right about something in the kitchen?" she joked.

Bay chuckled as she hurried up the stepstool, grabbed the stack of baking dishes and backed her way down to the floor, thankful she didn't keep her dress hems as low as most of the Amish women she knew. "Did you want all of these?"

"Actually, just the middle one." Anne leaned

against the counter, seeming a little out of breath.

As Bay fished out the rectangular baking dish, she glanced at Anne. "Are you okay? Maybe you should sit down."

"I'm fine." Anne gave a wave and then pressed her hand to her chest. "I'd forgotten what it was like, being this far along. Carrying a baby around twenty-four hours a day takes a lot of energy." Her smile was bittersweet, as if she was remembering her previous pregnancy, and maybe her husband.

Bay set the bright orange baking dish down in Anne's workspace on the counter. "Want me to put the others back?"

Anne shook her head. "No. Thanks. I'll find a better place for them. Just leave them on the counter there."

Bay did as she asked, and then folded up the stepstool. "Where does this go?"

"Oh, in the laundry room to the right of the dryer, but you don't need to do that. I'll do it in a second." Anne looked down at Matty, who was standing right in front of her now, looking up at her with obvious concern. "Mama's fine," she reassured him. "Oh my, look what Bay's brought. Are those homemade cinnamon rolls?" Her tone was obviously meant to distract her son and it worked.

Matty ran to the table to have a closer look at the treat.

Bay returned the stool to its place and walked back into the kitchen. "I hope you don't mind me just stopping by. I didn't have your phone number. I brought the cinnamon rolls to say thank-you." She reached into her denim jacket pocket. "And I brought back the socks and your scarf." She set them down beside the rolls.

"You don't need to call to stop by. Come anytime." Anne was still leaning against the kitchen counter, but her breath was more even. "I'm so glad you did, Bay. I don't have any friends nearby. All my church friends are farther away and can't just stop by. I'm hoping we can be friends." Her brow furrowed. "That's allowed, isn't it? Even though I'm Mennonite."

Bay laughed. "Of course. Why would that matter?"

Anne gave an exasperated smile. "Well, the church David and I grew up in…" She opened a drawer and pulled out a butter knife. "Our bishop thought Mennonites were fallen souls and we weren't to mingle with them." She gave a laugh as she crossed the kitchen to the table and took the plastic wrap off the rolls. "And you don't even want to know what he said about *Englishers*." She used the knife to cut out half a roll, pluck a napkin from a holder on the table and set the half piece in the middle of it. "Is this what you were waiting for?" she asked Matty.

He nodded, his eyes filled with excitement.

"Hop up in your chair, then." She set the treat at his place at the table and turned back to Bay. "I'm serious. Stop by anytime. The days are so long sometimes. I'd love the distraction."

Bay nibbled on her lower lip. "I think I'd like that."

"And I'll give you my phone number. You can call from your harness shop, right?"

"Sure can." Bay watched her open a kitchen drawer and pull out a pad and pen. "So my brothers and I came for our wagon, but it's not there anymore. I thought maybe David brought it up here, but… David's not home?" She hadn't seen his pickup but had hoped maybe it was parked somewhere out of sight.

"No, he went—oh my." Anne whipped around, covering her mouth with her hand. "I forgot. I'm sorry. I seem to get scatterbrained when I'm expecting." She sounded flustered now. "I was supposed to tell you if you showed up looking for the wagon that David got it out of the ditch at first light. He took it somewhere to be repaired. Something about the axle? He's got a big flatbed trailer, so he loaded it up and took off. He left a message at your family's harness shop this morning. Did you not get it? He called and talked to someone... Emily, I think?"

Bay rolled her eyes. She liked the young woman Benjamin had recently hired, but she wasn't entirely sure it would work out. Emily was an Amish girl who had just moved to Hickory Grove with her family. She was a nice girl, but what her mother called *whiffy*. Emily was friendly and comfortable with customers, *English* and Amish, but she wasn't much one for details. She never rang items correctly at the cash register, and she struggled to use the credit card machine. And she wasn't good about answering the phone. She either chatted with the caller about the weather and wasted time or totally got the message wrong if someone had a question she couldn't answer. Benjamin refused to let her go, though, no matter how many mistakes she made. His explanation was that the family needed the income, and he needed to share his financial blessings with others in the community.

"He took our wagon to be repaired?" Bay

asked, not sure if she should be pleased or annoyed. "He didn't have to do that."

Anne wrinkled her freckled nose. "I think he felt bad about what happened. That the spray from his truck startled your horse, and that's why you went in the ditch."

Because I accused him of causing the accident, Bay thought. Which was impulsive and just plain inaccurate. He hadn't done anything wrong. Horses shied sometimes.

"It wasn't his fault," Bay told Anne. "It just…happened."

"I think he was happy to do it." Anne moved the baking dish Bay had taken down for her, poured a little oil into it, and then used her fingers to spread it across the bottom and up the sides.

"Well…please thank him for me. And I guess he'll be in touch?" She glanced out the kitchen window to see her brothers in the wagon. They were laughing, which made her smile. "My brothers are waiting for me, so I'll say goodbye."

"Oh, I'm sorry you can't stay." Anne wiped her hand on a dish towel and turned to her. "Will you come again? I don't drive. Never learned." She gave a little laugh. "Matthew kept telling me I needed to learn and then…" Her tone was wistful, and when she met Bay's gaze, her eyes were teary. But she was still smiling.

Bay was surprised by the emotion she felt for this stranger. Anne was so strong, so brave. Bay couldn't imagine what it would be like to lose the man you loved, the father of your children. And she realized that she really did want to be friends with Anne. "I'll come back another day. I'll call you and—"

"Oh, you don't need to call. Come anytime. I never go anywhere but church. Poor David is even doing the grocery shopping these days."

Bay glanced at Matty, who had finished the half of the cinnamon roll on his plate. He was now eyeing the pan. "Goodbye, Matty. Maybe I'll see you in a few days."

The boy looked up and offered a shy smile.

"Wouldn't that be nice, Matty?" Anne asked. "If Bay came back to visit us?"

The boy remained silent, as his mother turned back to Bay. "I'll tell David you were here. I'm sure he'll give you a call or stop by your place, or something, once he knows what's going on with your wagon." Then she surprised Bay by throwing her arms around her.

The hug startled Bay, but then she wrapped her arms around Anne, feeling her rounded abdomen against her own flat one, and it felt…as if she had known her new friend her whole life.

Chapter Four

David had to fight his urge to beep his horn at the minivan in front of him. He understood the need to travel slower on the back roads and the importance of following the posted speed limits, but he didn't understand why people had to drive ten or fifteen miles an hour *under* the speed limit.

He was tempted to pass, but there was a double yellow line because of the road curves, and he wasn't about to get a ticket. He'd had his driver's license almost ten years now, and he didn't have a single ticket; he wasn't about to change that.

He would just have to be patient. He reminded himself of Paul's words in his letter to the Romans. *Patience in tribulation.*

And ordinarily, he *was* a patient man. One had to be, in the greenhouse business. With almost everything he did, whether it was growing perennial flowers, trees or bushes, there were times when action was required by him, and other times when he just had to sit back and wait. Patience was required while the plants germinated from seed, while they grew sturdy enough to be replanted in larger pots. And even once there were healthy plants, one had to be patient while they grew fruits or vegetables, while those fruits and vegetables ripened, or while flowers reached full bloom.

The problem was he wasn't feeling patient today. He wanted to get home in case Bay stopped by. He'd meant to be home more than an hour ago, but it had taken him longer than he'd anticipated at Jared Kline's house, where he'd taken Bay's wagon to be mended. In his early sixties, Jared was a kind man from their church who had been happy to fix the broken axle for free to return a favor David had done for him. But Jared reminded him of his uncle Adam—a nice man who could. Not. Stop. Talking.

Jared chatted about the weather, his neighbor's sheep, and his wife's cousin's friend who, at seventy-eight years old, had fallen from a tree she was climbing. He talked about the leak in his hose that ran to his washing machine, and the flavor of toothpaste he preferred. Honestly, after forty-five minutes of not saying more than ten words, David had been ready to just load Bay's wagon back on his trailer and take it elsewhere. Then, just as he finally escaped from Jared, he received a text from Anne asking that he stop at the drugstore for her. How could he tell her no, that he wanted to get home just in case this smart, attractive, single woman happened to stop by? A woman he had no chance with?

He couldn't. So, even though he had been halfway home when Anne texted him, he'd backtracked, gone to the drugstore and then taken every shortcut he knew home. He could almost see his driveway now. He saw the roof of one of his greenhouses in the distance. He was almost to the house, and maybe, just maybe, Bay would be there.

But the white van seemed to have slowed down even further. David could have walked faster than the minivan, even pulling his flatbed trailer with a few lengths of corn string and muscle.

Once he'd taken the curve at a snail's pace and could see his driveway, David checked his rearview mirror, saw all was clear, and hit the accelerator. He passed the minivan on two solid yellow lines and wheeled into his driveway. He was half expecting—or at least half wishing—that Bay would be there, but why would she? He'd left a message at her stepfather's harness shop first thing that morning, letting her know he had gotten the wagon out of the ditch and that it was being repaired. In the message, he'd asked the young girl who answered the phone to tell Bay that he'd contact her as soon as he knew when the wagon would be fixed.

With no sign of an Amish vehicle, David parked in front of what had once been a dairy barn. Because he didn't have cows, it was now home to three horses, four goats and a passel of barn cats. With a glance around to see that all was well in the barnyard, he hurried across the driveway toward the house, the bag from the drugstore in his hand.

"Hello?" he called as he closed the back door behind him. From the doorway between the laundry room and the kitchen, he saw Anne sweeping. Matty sat at the kitchen table coloring with crayons. It smelled like she'd been baking. There was a hint of cinnamon in the air.

"Boots off!" Anne warned. "I just swept. Your slippers are in your cubby."

David impatiently stepped out of his boots, shrugged off his barn coat and walked into the kitchen in his socks. "You hear from Bay?" He set the bag on the kitchen table and pressed a kiss to the top of Matty's head. The boy was drawing circles, filling the whole page with them.

"She was here. You just missed her."

Disappointment washed over him. "She was here?"

"She came looking for the wagon."

"She was looking for the wagon?"

Anne stopped sweeping and leaned on her broom. "Is there an echo in this kitchen?" she teased, knitting her brow.

"She didn't get my message?" he asked.

"She didn't get your message."

He chuckled, shaking his head as he realized his sister was doing the same thing he had done. "Yup. Definitely an echo in here."

Anne laughed and tried to lean over, broom in one hand, the dustpan in the other, so she could gather the dry cereal from Matty's breakfast off the floor.

David only had to watch her struggle with her belly in the way for a couple of seconds before he took the dustpan from her. He had no problem sweeping the kitchen, but he knew better than to try to get her to pass the broom to him. His little sister by eighteen months didn't get angry often, but when she did… David preferred not to be the recipient of that anger.

"I guess the message didn't reach Bay before she left her house. She and her two brothers came for the wagon, didn't find it in the ditch, and came here looking for it."

He carried the dustpan to the trash and dumped it. "I knew I should have left a note or something," he fretted.

Anne laughed as she took the dustpan from him and carried them to the mudroom, where she kept them behind the door. "You were going to leave a note in a *ditch*?" she asked.

He ignored her. "What did she say?"

"What do you mean, what did she say?" Anne returned to the kitchen. "She said she'd come for the wagon, and I told her you'd taken it to be repaired."

"That's it?"

Anne shrugged and went to the sink and began to wash the breakfast dishes. "She apologized for stopping by without calling. I told her she was welcome anytime. She needn't call ahead. I really like her. I think we could be good friends."

"She say anything about me?" The moment the words were out of his mouth, he wished he could take them back. He sounded like a teenage boy.

Anne giggled and glanced over her shoulder at him. "Like how handsome and smart and strong you are?"

He opened his eyes wider, not sure how to respond. *Did she really say those things? Was she attracted to him in the same way he was attracted to her?*

Before he could figure out how to answer, Anne turned back to the sink, laughing again. "No, she didn't say anything like that."

Not realizing he'd been holding his breath, he exhaled, trying to see the humor in his little sister's joke. "Very funny."

She was still chuckling to herself as she set a clean bowl in the dish drain. "Oh, but she did bring those cinnamon rolls for us. For you, really, I guess. As a thank-you. Did you tell her how much you like homemade cinnamon rolls? They even have lots of icing, just the way you like them."

Only then did David notice the aluminum foil tray with a plastic lid on top sitting on the table. "I don't think we talked about cinnamon rolls." He lifted the plastic lid and inhaled. There was the cinnamon he'd been smelling. "Wow." He glanced at Matty. "Hey, little man, did you see a burglar here?" He looked one way and then the other as if searching for a masked man. "Because someone stole half of one of my cinnamon rolls."

Matty smirked but kept his head down, licking at the evidence of the white icing on the corners of his mouth. Now he was coloring in the circles he'd drawn all over the piece of paper.

David pried the other half of the roll out and took a big bite. "Mmm," he muttered, closing his eyes. "These might be the best cinnamon rolls I've ever eaten."

"You know what it means when a woman bakes for a man, don't you? It means she likes you, as in *likes you*."

David felt his cheeks grow warm with embarrassment. "I suspect she was just being nice."

Anne crossed her arms across her chest and leaned against the kitchen cabinet. "Men can be so daft. You have to see the subtle hints," she told him conspiratorially. "There was no need for her to come here this morning. Her brothers could have gotten the wagon. And the fact that she made you cinnamon rolls, which is yeast bread and time-consuming?" She lifted her brows. "She likes you."

He grabbed a paper napkin from the table and wiped his mouth. "You think?"

She nodded, smiling.

"So what do I do?" he asked, feeling like that schoolboy again.

"You can start by letting her know what's going on with her wagon."

He stroked his clean-shaven face. "You think I should call the harness shop and ask to speak to her."

Anne laughed. "No, silly goose. You should go to her place and tell her personally." She looked at Matty. "Your uncle David, he's a silly goose, isn't he?"

The boy nodded soberly.

"I should go?" David asked. "Now?"

"What else do you have to do?" she asked, hanging a dish towel with a rooster on it on the oven door.

"I don't know, my to-do list is about this long." He stretched out his arms. "And at the top of the list is fixing the drippy faucet in the downstairs bath. You've been asking me to do it for a week."

She gave a wave. "The faucet can wait."

"Are you sure?" he asked, but he was already heading for the door.

"Go!" Anne called after him. "Tell Bay I said hi and not to be a stranger."

David grabbed his boots in the laundry room doorway, stepped over their resident mama cat, and went to the bench near the door to pull on the boots. "Will do."

"And ask Bay to marry you while you're at it," Anne called.

David didn't dignify that with an answer.

Using the register counter as a desk in the greenhouse shop, Bay signed a check she'd written to one of the distributors where she bought plastic growing trays. She licked the envelope, sealed it and added her address and a stamp. There had been a mix-up with the bill, and she wanted to get the payment in the mail as quickly as possible. She checked the clock on the wall. It was nearly noon. If she hurried, she might make it to the mailbox at the end of their driveway before the mail carrier reached it.

"Joshua?" she called to her stepbrother, who was working in the attached greenhouse. He was planting tiny annual flower plants they'd grown themselves from seed. "I'm going to run down to the mailbox. When I get back, I'll mix up the fertilizer."

"Sounds good," he hollered. "The sun's peeking out, finally. Take your time."

Bay slipped into a quilted denim jacket that had once belonged to one of Benjamin's sons. With so many patches on it and a torn cuff, it had been relegated to the rag box her mother kept in her sewing room. Bay had snitched it from the box, making it her own. While she would never be seen off the farm in a ratty men's coat, it was perfect for working in the greenhouse. It was warm and durable and big enough to wear a sweater under it. After fastening the hook and eyes, she picked up the envelope and walked out the shop's door, a little bell jingling overhead.

In the parking lot the greenhouse shared with the harness shop, she spotted two pickup trucks and a horse and buggy. Customers. One of the trucks was white, and for an instant, she *hoped* it might be David's. Which was silly, of course. He was a busy man with his business, and the farm and his sister and nephew to care for. If he had a message to pass on about their wagon, he'd call the harness shop the way he had that morning. And he'd probably ask to speak to Benjamin. After all, it was *his* wagon she'd borrowed. And wrecked. But true to form, her stepfather hadn't been the least bit upset when he heard about the accident. In fact, when she'd arrived home after the incident, he'd given her a big hug, telling how thankful he was that she hadn't been hurt. He told her that wagons and sadly even horses could be replaced, but his Bay never could be. He'd also dismissed her attempt to offer to pay for damages, telling her it hurt his feelings that she would say such a thing.

Reaching the lane that had recently been covered with several inches of fresh oyster shells, Bay turned right, the farmhouse where they lived behind her. Just as Joshua had said, the sun was out at last, and she closed her eyes for a moment, lifting her chin so she could feel its radiant warmth.

It had been a cold winter for Delaware, and then spring had been late in coming. But the temperatures were supposed to continue to rise the rest of the week, with Saturday predicted to be in the sixties. With Easter behind them, she and Joshua hoped the warm weather was just around the corner, but having grown up in upstate New York, she was hesitant to make any predictions. She knew from experience that just when you declared winter to be over, there would be snow again, piled up to the windowsills.

But winter *seemed* to be over. The thunderstorm the previous day was evidence of that, wasn't it? You didn't see thunderstorms in the winter. The idea that spring had finally arrived excited her. Spring was when plants that lay dormant all winter began to spring forth from the soil, when the leaves would pop out in the trees and bushes, and daffodils, tulips and hyacinths would poke from the soil. She had already spotted her *mam's* crocuses in the flower beds around the house.

It was a good quarter of a mile down the lane to the road, but Bay didn't mind the walk. It gave her time to think without worrying about making any mistakes in her woolgathering. The other day while stewing over a conversation with her twin, Ginger, about why she was not attending a frolic at the matchmaker's in Seven Poplars, she'd accidentally mixed marigold seeds with cosmos and now the seeds were in an envelope waiting to be planted in her mother's garden. And two weeks ago, after her mother expressed her disappointment when Bay didn't accept an offer for a ride home with an *eligible* young man, Bay had been so unfocused that she'd combined the wrong ratio of ground limestone to sphagnum peat moss while making potting soil. Such a mistake might seem trivial to a non-gardener, but potting soil that was too alkaline would prevent plants from absorbing nutrients properly. And they would die or grow so spindly that they would have to be thrown in the compost heap.

Halfway to the road, Bay leaned down to

pick up a discarded soda pop can. She crumpled it in her hand and stuffed it in her jacket pocket. She didn't understand littering. Who did people who tossed cans into driveways think was going to pick it up?

The sound of a vehicle approaching caught Bay's attention, and she looked up to see the mail carrier speeding past the driveway. She took off at a run, waving the envelope. "Wait!" she cried.

As the postal carrier stuck out her hand to take the envelope, Bay caught sight, out of the corner of her eye, of a white pickup truck signaling to turn into their lane. At first, she thought it was David. But it was undoubtedly just her imagination. In a day, dozens of white pickups came down their driveway headed for the harness shop. And once the greenhouse opened for business in three weeks, the number would double. "Thank you!" she told the mail carrier, out of breath.

The mail carrier plucked the envelope from Bay's hand. "Want the mail?" she asked, all business. They had two mail carriers, one during the week and a different one on weekends. Joe, the weekend carrier, who had to be seventy, was friendly and chatty. But Jazzy, a pretty woman in her forties with little braids all over her head, never said anything more than was necessary.

"Sure. Yes, thank you." As Bay accepted the bundle wrapped in a rubber band, she realized that the man driving the white pickup had red hair. A second later, she recognized him.

It was David!

And he was headed up the drive. A moment of panic overtook Bay, and she froze. The mail truck took off, throwing bits of gravel onto her sneakers. David must not have seen her, his view blocked by the mail truck. She couldn't let him see her looking like this, in a man's old, patched coat and her hair covered with a stained headscarf. Maybe she could just wait until he reached the parking lot, and then she could cut across the lawn and run around the back of the shop, and he'd never see her.

But she didn't want David going up to the harness shop. She didn't want him talking to Benjamin or her siblings, or even the whiffy Emily at the shop's register. She didn't know why; she only knew that she didn't.

"David!" she hollered, taking off after his truck. "David!"

He must have either heard her or seen her in his mirror because he hit his brakes. Bay had to hit her own to keep from running right into the back door of his truck. "David," she repeated.

His window was down. "Bay." He smiled as he shifted into Park.

"What—" She was trying to catch her breath without appearing to be out of it. "What…are you doing here?"

He had a big smile for her, so big that she couldn't resist smiling back. He was looking at her the way she had seen men look at her friends. The way a man looked at a woman when he liked her in a romantic way. The idea was scary and exciting at the same time.

"I came to see you."

"Oh," she exhaled.

He rested his forearm on the open window and leaned out a bit. "I guess you didn't get my message I left this morning. I talked to Emily."

"New hire," she answered. "Sorry about that. She's still working on her phone skills."

He chuckled. "Well, sorry you ended up coming for the wagon and not finding it. I guess I didn't think the whole thing through. A friend from church is a retired welder, and he has all the equipment in his garage. There's an issue with the wagon's axle, but he says it's an easy fix, though you might need a new wheel, too. Depends on whether or not he can straighten it out. He says he doesn't see many wheels with rolled steel tires."

"*Ya*, my stepfather brought it from New York when we moved here. I think it was his father's."

David nodded appreciatively. "Well, my friend Jared says the wagon is definitely worth saving. It will probably be next week before he gets it done, though. I hope that's okay?"

He was wearing aviator sunglasses, a blue plaid flannel shirt, and one of those goose down puffy vests *Englishers* wore. But he didn't look like an *Englisher*. There was something about his face that was very... wholesome. She wondered exactly how old he was.

"I know, I should have checked with you first," David continued. "But when I called Jared, he said he could do it, and since it was free, I figured, why not?"

"No, no. It's fine." She hugged the bundle of mail, hoping he didn't notice the trash sticking out of her pocket. Or the old clothing she was wearing. He didn't seem to, or maybe he just didn't care. That idea appealed to her. That maybe he was smiling at her because he liked who she was, not what she looked like.

"Benjamin was tickled you found someone to look at the wagon because we don't have an Amish wheelwright around here anymore. There used to be one over in Seven Poplars but I guess that family moved to Kentucky last year."

"We had a wheelwright where I grew up in Wisconsin. He was good at his trade, but he was the crankiest man." David chuckled at the memory.

And Bay found herself smiling again. And for a moment, they were quiet, but it wasn't an uncomfortable silence.

David then tapped the door with his hand. "Hey, I want you to know how much I appreciate you offering a hand in friendship to my sister. Yesterday at supper she mentioned that it was nice to make a friend who didn't know her before Matthew died."

"Why's that?" Bay asked.

He took his time to answer and Bay appreciated that he thought before he spoke, something she was working on. She also liked that he could talk on a matter that involved feelings. She didn't often find that in men her own age.

"She feels like you want to be friends because of who she is. Not because you feel sorry for her."

Bay mulled that over. "I do feel empathy for her. I've never been married so I realize that I don't know what it's like to lose a husband." She met his gaze. "But I lost my father, so I know what it's like to lose someone you love, someone who is the center of your life." She shrugged. "But I just like her. And... I think I like her because, in some ways, she's different than anyone else I know. All of my friends are Amish." She wrinkled her nose. "Is that a terrible thing to say?"

He laughed. "It's not. I understand exactly what you mean. And even though you're Amish and we're Mennonite, because we all grew up Amish, I think we have a lot of things in common. Like having faith in the center of our lives."

Bay noticed that he was saying *we* now. "Because *we* grew up Amish..." Hearing him say that made her feel good—the idea that they both wanted to be friends with her.

He tapped the truck door with his hand again. "What are you doing today?"

His steady gaze made her slightly uncomfortable, but not in a bad way. It was a feeling she didn't recall experiencing before. "Me? Oh... I'm... I was mailing a check to one of our distributors. Getting the mail." She motioned to the bundle she held against her chest. "And my brother Joshua is replanting seedlings we grew from seed. Vinca, zinnias and geraniums, I think. When I get back, I'm going to mix up fertilizer."

"What do you use?"

Feeling less self-conscious talking about gardening rather than herself, she rattled the ingredients off the top of her head. "Gypsum, seed meal, dolomite lime and ag lime."

"You add bonemeal to that or kelp meal?" he asked.

"Both."

"So you use a dry fertilizer," he remarked thoughtfully. "I use liquid and dry. Depends on what I need it for. Of course, I don't grow annuals. Well, I haven't in the past. Though I think there's decent money in it around here, especially if you can sell them to the big-box stores." He glanced away, out the windshield, then back at her. "I'm kind of fascinated with hydroponic growing. I think it would be amazing to grow and sell annual flower and vegetable plants without soil."

"I don't know anything about hydroponics, but I'm intrigued by the idea of it, too," she told him. Without thinking, in her enthusiasm, she took a step closer to the window. "I've never seen hydroponic growing, but I've read all about it. And seen pictures.

Joshua and I subscribe to a couple of commercial gardening magazines, and of course, I see the supplies in the sales catalogs. My *mam* says I'm the only woman she knows who reads gardening catalogs for fun. My sisters read every issue of *The Budget* front to back. That's an Amish newspaper."

"Annie says the same thing about me. And we get *The Budget*, too. Because it's a way for us to keep up with what's going on with friends all over the country. Annie reads it mostly, though. Does anyone grow hydroponically commercially around here?"

She shook her head. "I don't think so. I imagine you make money at it, though. People around here are really into organic growing. And anything progressive. And they're willing to pay a steeper price. My sister Lovey sells cage-free eggs, charges a dollar more a carton and she's got more customers than eggs."

He was quiet for a second, then he looked up at her again. "I talked to a guy on the phone the other day in Sussex County who's growing hydroponically. He invited me to come to see his greenhouse. What would you think about going with me? You know, to check out his operation, get an idea of the cost of setup and such."

Bay didn't take the time to think the invitation through or its consequences. "I would love that!" she told him, practically bouncing in her sneakers.

"You would?" He looked surprised. And pleased. "Okay, then." He was grinning, looking as excited as Bay felt. "Ronny—he's the grower—mentioned next Thursday. Would that work for you? Because if it doesn't, I could call him and reschedule for a better day."

"Nope. Next Thursday would be great."

"Okay, then. I guess I'll see you Thursday. Want me to pick you up?"

"How about if I come by your place?" The words came out of her mouth before she could think better of them. Of the whole idea of going somewhere with David. Alone. Something her mother might frown on and the town gossip would love. An unmarried Amish woman going somewhere unchaperoned with a single Mennonite man. That would be fodder for chatter for weeks in their little community. "I promised Anne I'd stop by next week, anyway," she added.

"Okay, well…" He seemed hesitant to go. "I guess I'll just turn around here and head home. I've got a list of things a mile long to do. Good talking to you."

"Good talking to you, too." Bay stepped back into the grass and watched David turn around in his truck in the driveway. He put down the passenger side window as he slowly passed her. "See you next week!"

"See you next week!" Bay waved and watched him pull out onto the blacktop before turning to head back to the greenhouse.

She couldn't believe she'd agreed to go with him. Talk about impulsive. What was even harder to believe was that she had decided so quickly that she didn't want her mother to know about it. But her mother would never understand why she would want to see plants being grown hydroponically because she didn't understand Bay's passion for growing plants. And she might insist that Bay take one of her sisters or a brother as chaperone.

Of course, chaperones were only needed for dates. And this wasn't a date.

At least she didn't think it was…

As David pulled onto the blacktop, he glanced into the rearview mirror. Bay was still standing there in her driveway, watching him go. And smiling. Which made him smile.

With his eyes on the road ahead, he gripped the steering wheel. Did I just make a date? he wondered. *With Bay?*

Well, maybe it wasn't exactly a *date* date. But they were two single people going together somewhere, so it certainly could be a date. If that was what he wanted it to be.

But surely Bay didn't think it was a date. She was Amish. He wasn't. It wasn't done, he reminded himself.

A horse and wagon with an Amish man driving went by in the opposite direction. He waved at David, and David waved back. A neighbor probably.

David liked the idea that the man who had waved might be a neighbor. Even though David had moved from Wisconsin to Delaware four months ago, he had still felt like he was here visiting. He told himself he hadn't made any friends because he was busy, because he hadn't been here that long yet. But if he was truthful with himself, the fact was that he hadn't really gone out of his way to meet anyone. He didn't really talk much to the people he *did* meet. Because he really hadn't wanted to move, maybe he had been resisting the idea of it, even now that he was here.

After his brother-in-law died, he had seriously considered insisting Annie and Matty come to live with him in Wisconsin. And if she had agreed to it, that was probably where they would be now. But Anne had stubbornly

refused. She had said she didn't want to up-
root her son and leave her home, church and
friends, especially not when she was expecting. He'd even enlisted the help of friends and
relatives to try to convince Anne to move, but
she'd still refused to give in. Everyone they
knew had thought it would be foolish for him
to pick up and move just because Anne didn't
want to leave Delaware, but after many days
of prayer, David felt led to come.

At the time when he made the choice to sell
his place and move, he had told himself that if
it wasn't God beckoning him to Kent County,
Delaware, then it was his sense of responsibility to his sister and her family. Now he
wondered, as he turned onto his road, if God
wanted him to move to Delaware to meet Bay.

Chapter Five

The following week Bay climbed up into the antique courting buggy her stepbrother Levi had restored, as her *mam* watched her, frowning with obvious disapproval. Her mother and sisters didn't like the two-seater and felt it was unsafe, especially for a young woman. It was so lightweight in comparison to the bigger, enclosed family buggies that they thought it bounced around too much and it was easy to go too fast.

Bay liked it because she *could* go fast, especially with Levi and Eve's new gelding. Joe was a retired racehorse, but at only five years old, he could still fly down the road. Bay loved the feel of the wind in her face and the motion of the buggy as it sailed over the pavement and the trees and fields streaked by.

"I appreciate you running the potpie and

biscuits over to Ginger," her mother said from the ground. She stood with her arms crossed over her chest. "I just wish you'd take one of the other buggies, or at least Sassafras, instead of this troublemaker." She lifted her chin at the gelding that was dancing in his traces, as excited as Bay was to be headed for the open road.

"I'm sure Ginger will appreciate not having to make supper tonight," Bay responded, wishing the horse would behave itself, at least until they got out of her *mam's* sight. "I know she has to be worn out, what with the new baby and the four other little ones. I don't know how she does it, and always with a smile on her face."

Bay's twin had married their widowed neighbor with four children, and now she and Eli had a *kinner* of their own. Just thinking about running a household with so many children and responsibilities made Bay think maybe she wasn't meant to be a mother and wife. But Ginger had taken all of the changes in her life in stride. She never seemed overwhelmed and she always had a smile on her face. She had stepped into motherhood as if it were a comfortable dress she had been wearing her whole life.

"How does Ginger manage it all? Love,

that's how she does it," their mother answered
simply. "Love for Eli, for the children, for
God."

"I suppose it's hard to understand when I'm
not in her place," Bay commented.

"Ya." Her mother stepped back. "Give Ginger my love. And my grandchildren, too. Tell
your sister I'll see her Thursday for the quilting circle she's hosting." She tightened the
knot of her headscarf at the nape of her neck.
"Are you going with me? You haven't said.
Tara and Nettie are."

Thursday, she was going with David. Bay
took the reins firmly in her gloved hands,
avoiding eye contact. *"Ne,* I wasn't planning
on it."

Her mother frowned. "I suppose it was
foolish of me to ask. I know you avoid sewing like I do the dentist." She sighed. "But
these days, a woman doesn't have to sew her
own bedding, does she? It can be bought. And
whoever you wed may not have a homemade
quilt on his bed, but at least he'll have beautiful flowers in his window boxes."

Bay smiled, appreciating her mother's
words, which also made her feel guilty. She
knew it was wrong to keep her trip with
David from her mother, but wasn't she too
old to be asking permission from her par-

ents for anything? Ginger certainly didn't ask them. Everyone assumed that because Ginger was married with children, she could make her own choices. It wasn't fair. But it was the way it was in their community.

"I'll give Ginger a hug from you. I promise! And kisses for all of the children, whether they want them or not. See you later." Bay gave Joe some rein and the horse leaped forward, causing the buggy to lurch and sway as they pulled into the lane that led to the road.

As Bay pulled away, her mother gave a loud *tut* of disapproval, but Bay didn't look back. She held the reins firmly, thankful for the old gloves that Levi had given her. The first time she had taken the courting buggy out, she'd returned with blisters on her hands from the leather reins and the gelding's enthusiasm. Her sister Tara had fussed over her like a mother hen, and then when Bay had refused the balm she offered, Tara had run to their mother to say she didn't think Bay ought to be driving that wild beast.

Bay sailed past the harness shop and her greenhouse, oyster shell from the driveway flying in every direction. Seeing there was no traffic on the country road, she turned onto the blacktop road toward Ginger's without stopping.

Bay loved Tara, but they were so different that she sometimes struggled to understand her. And she knew that Tara felt the same way about her. But the thing was, despite only being twenty-one, Tara knew who she was and exactly what she wanted in life. And Bay didn't. And that was causing the distance in their relationship. Of course, that could be said for all of Bay's relationships right now. No one in her family understood her. Except maybe Joshua, who loved her for who she was and kept telling her that God would reveal her place in His world and that she only had to be patient.

Patience was not one of Bay's virtues.

She laughed and gave Joe a little more rein as they reached the center of a curve, and the horse stretched his long neck and went even faster.

An hour later, Bay was back in the courting buggy. Her nephew, Simon, now ten years old, untied Joe from the hitching post in their yard. Ginger stood on the steps of her porch, baby Paul on her hip.

"You should come to the quilting on Thursday," Ginger called to her.

"I can't," Bay answered.

"You don't have to sew. I just want you to be here. I miss you, *Schweschder*."

The moment the gelding realized the boy had released him, he started to back up, moving so quickly that Bay was afraid he would turn over the buggy. "Careful, Simon," Bay called as she tugged on the reins. "Easy, boy. Easy there, Joe." She made the gelding walk in a circle, moving them closer to the house.

"I know you don't like children, but they really are well-behaved," Ginger said, emotion in her voice. "And we can always send them outside to play now that it's getting warmer. Except for this one," she added, bouncing Paul, who was wearing a long white dress and baby bonnet.

"Who said I didn't like children?" Bay worked the reins, trying to make the gelding hold still. "I never said I didn't like children. I… I'm busy, Ginger. With the business. Joshua and I are a week behind our repotting and we want to open by Mother's Day." As exasperated with her sister as the horse, she took a deep breath. "I'm not coming because I have somewhere else to be."

"Oh, where are you going?" Ginger asked. "Somewhere fun, I hope. You work too much."

Finally, the gelding settled, and Bay gave her twin her full attention. She pressed her lips together, contemplating whether or not to say anything about David. Ginger would never tattle on her, unlike Tara or Nettie, but Bay didn't know if she wanted to share the news of her budding friendship with David and his sister or not. But she was so excited about seeing the hydroponic greenhouses with him that she wanted to tell *someone*.

"If I tell you where I'm going, you can't tell *Mam*. Or anyone else. *Oll recht?*"

Ginger narrowed her gaze as she came down the steps. "Is it something dangerous? You know *Mam's* rule. We all have a right to privacy, but not if it involves something dangerous. I know you and Jacob were talking about how you'd like to skydive someday…"

Bay laughed. "I'm not going skydiving. I'm going to look at greenhouses where someone is growing fruits and vegetables hydroponically. In water rather than soil."

"I know what hydroponic means." Ginger reached the bottom step but stayed there, safely out of the way of Joe's hooves. "Who are you going with?"

Bay glanced into the barnyard, where Ginger's boys were chasing each other, throwing bits of straw and laughing. She looked back at her sister. "The brother of a new friend." She hesitated. "They're Mennonite. But they grew up Amish," she added quickly. As if that made a difference.

"Recht." Ginger drew out the word. "And is this brother a single man?" She raised her brows.

"Ya."

Ginger nodded. "I agree, you shouldn't tell *Mam*."

"That's what I decided. There's no need to worry her." Bay shrugged. "It's just a ride to Sussex County and back. I'll be back before *Mam* is home from your quilting."

Ginger kissed the top of her baby's head and said cautiously, "You need to be careful, *Schweschder.*"

"He's a good man, Ginger."

"I'm sure he is, but you know what *Mam* always told us. A woman can't fall in love with a man she doesn't know. That's why you stay away from single men who aren't acceptable husband material."

Their gazes met and Bay understood the warning. "Well, I don't think anyone needs to worry about me falling in love," she said. "It's just that David owns commercial greenhouses and he has the same interests I do. And he doesn't care that I'm a girl running a business. He doesn't see a problem with that."

"David, is it?" Ginger said thoughtfully.

Then she inhaled and slowly let out her breath. "Promise me you'll be careful."

Bay rolled her eyes. "I'm an excellent judge of character. He's a good person. I'll be perfectly safe with him. And his sister will know where we're going and when we'll be back, and I trust her, too."

Just then, one of the boys began to howl and Ginger and Bay both looked his way.

"Oww, Mama! He's a bad boy." Phillip cried in Pennsylvania *Deitsch*, holding his eye. "I got straw in my eye. Andrew threw it at me." He leaned down and grabbed a handful of straw that was blowing across the yard and threw it at his brother.

Ginger looked at Bay and sighed. "Sorry, I best take care of this."

"It's okay." Bay lifted the reins. "See you soon?" she called as the courting buggy began to roll forward.

"See you soon," Ginger called after her as she walked across the yard. "And be careful!"

Bay smiled as she flew down the driveway toward the road. She was glad she had told Ginger about David. It felt good to share her happiness with someone else.

When Bay reached the road and pulled to a stop to look for cars, it crossed her mind that she could as easily take the long way home.

And if she felt like it, she could stop in at David's and say hi to Anne and Matty. She had promised Anne she'd visit again. This was the perfect opportunity.

Bay urged the gelding onto the road in the direction of David's place. Who was she kidding? She wanted to see Anne and Matty, but she wanted to see David, too, and maybe he would just happen to be there. Then she wouldn't have to wait until Thursday to see him. The thought of getting to see him, maybe talking business, made her grin and give the gelding more rein.

Half an hour later, Bay was at David and Anne's back door. There was no sight of David's white truck in the barnyard and she tried not to feel disappointed as she knocked on the door.

When it opened, Matty was standing there looking up at her solemnly. "Hi, Matty," she said. "Is your mama here?"

He nodded and opened the door.

"Bay!" Anne greeted as Bay walked into the kitchen. "I'm so glad you came! I was afraid you would think I was being polite when I told you to stop anytime. You made my day!" She was wearing a plain dress that looked very similar to Bay's, but with a flowered apron tied around her rounded belly, and instead of a prayer *kapp*, she was wearing a bit of lace pinned to the back of her hair tied up in a bun.

"I was out delivering a meal to my sister Ginger. She has a new baby and four small children, so my *mam* likes to give her a break once in a while from cooking."

"Oh, how nice," Anne sighed. "I'd love a break from cooking. But right now I need a break from cleaning. I was making myself some tea. Want some? We have fresh blueberry muffins, too, don't we, Matty?" She looked around. "Where did he go? He was here a minute ago."

"Down the hall, I think." Bay walked toward the kitchen counter. "How about if I make our tea and you sit down and rest for a minute."

"You sound like David."

Bay laughed and began to fill the kettle with water from the tap the way she had seen Anne do it. They didn't have an electric kettle in their home, of course, but Benjamin had bought one recently and set up a coffee and tea station in the shop. At first, it had been for customers, but now the entire family and employees were enjoying, too.

"Your brother's right. You need to get off your feet and rest." Bay wanted to ask her where David was, but she didn't want Anne to think she had only come to see him.

"Fine," Anne surrendered, dropping into one of the kitchen chairs. "Tea bags are in the canister on the counter." She pointed to a pretty crockery tub with a lid on it. "Mugs are in the top cabinet to the right of the sink."

Bay set the kettle back on its plate and flipped the switch to turn it on. She carried two mugs to the table and sat down across from Anne.

Anne leaned back in the chair and groaned with obvious pleasure as she rubbed her extended abdomen. "Oh, this feels so good. My feet are swollen." She propped them up on the seat of the chair beside her to reveal fuzzy pink slippers. "That's even better," she sighed with enjoyment.

At the sound of little footsteps, they both looked in the direction of the hall, from where Matty appeared. He was holding several books in his arms.

"Oh no," Anne groaned and looked at Bay. "You don't have to. Really."

"I don't have to do what?" Bay watched Matty walk around the table and come to her, not his mother.

The little boy looked up at her with his big brown eyes and offered the stack of books, which she could tell by his face were a great treasure to him.

"You want me to read you a book?" Bay asked, surprised he would come to her. It made her feel good, because no matter what her sister had said, she really *did* like children.

Matty nodded.

Bay glanced at Anne.

"You can if you want to, but really—" her new friend held up her hand "—you don't have to. I read to him several times a day and David reads to him for an hour every night."

"I want to." Bay looked down at Matty and put out her hands to accept the precious picture books. "Let's see what you have here," she said to the boy. She set the stack on the table and thumbed through them. "*Summertime in the Big Woods, Winter on the Farm, Going to Town.*" She chuckled. "They're all Laura Ingalls Wilder books." Bay and her sisters had read the chapter books as little girls, quite progressive for their mother to allow it. What books Amish children could read was limited: nothing with undesirable *Englisher* ways, no animated animals that could talk, and nothing that went against the church's teachings.

"I don't know why, but he loves these

books." Annie went on to explain how her son had become attached to and obsessed with the picture books after his father died. "You ought to be pleased that he's asking you to read to him. It means he likes you. He hasn't taken to strangers since Matthew died. It took him weeks to warm up to David."

"Okay, let me get your mother some tea and then I'll read to you," Bay told Matty. She got up and made tea for them both and, as per Anne's instructions, poured a cup of milk for the boy. Then she took plates out for the muffins and sat down again. "Do you want to sit on my lap while I read, or do you want to sit on the chair?" she asked Matty.

He pulled out the chair beside her and climbed up.

"*Oll recht*, I think that means you'll be sitting beside me." Bay glanced at Anne for confirmation and Annie smiled back, obviously pleased Bay was willing to read to her son. "Here we go," Bay told Matty, taking the book on the top of the stack.

Anne chuckled and peeled the paper off a blueberry muffin. "You're going to regret this," she warned, her tone teasing but kind and full of obvious love for her son.

Bay read a book to Matty. And then another. And another. She was ready to begin a fourth when she heard the back door open. David called from the mudroom, "Thank you for reading *Going to Town*. I don't think I have it in me to read it again today."

He appeared in the doorway in his stocking feet. "Bay, good to see you. Nice horse and buggy you've got out there." He hooked his thumb in the general direction. "Is that yours? I have to say it suits you better than the wagon and the old mare."

Bay felt herself blush. "It's my brother Levi's. He's a buggy maker. He found the buggy at an auction somewhere in Maryland and rebuilt it. It's an antique."

"Well, it's beautiful and I'm impressed that you can handle that gelding. That horse is spirited—I could see it in his eyes." He shifted his attention to Anne. "Are those blueberry muffins I smell?"

"They came out of the oven half an hour ago," Anne replied. "Would you like some tea?" She started to get up. "I can—"

"Anne," he interrupted, holding up a hand to stop her. "Please sit down. This must be the first time you've sat since you got up at dawn. She stands eating breakfast half the time," he told Bay before turning back to his sister. "What have I done to make you think I'm incapable of making my own coffee?"

Anne relaxed in the chair. "Tea," she corrected.

"What?" David looked at her, not following. "I was going to have coffee."

"No, you're not," she told him. "You had three cups this morning, which is one cup beyond your limit. You're cut off. No more maple syrup for that one today." She pointed at her son. "And no more coffee for you."

Watching this exchange, Bay had to press her lips together to suppress a laugh. She loved how David and Anne bickered the way she and her siblings did. Despite their minor disagreements, they obviously loved each other dearly.

"Fine, I'll have tea, Miss Bossy," David told Annie, then he looked at Bay. "I see the little man tricked you into reading to him. Let me guess. Two books?"

Bay grinned back. "Three."

"When Bay arrived, he went right to his room and brought her the books," Anne explained, gesturing to her son. "I have no idea what's gotten into him. He's been sitting there beside her ever since. What's gotten into you, Matty?"

The boy said nothing.

"Wow." David turned on the teakettle. "You should feel honored he trusts you, Bay.

He's a good judge of character, though." And then David winked at Bay. Just like the day she had met him.

Was he flirting with her right in front of his sister? A warmth of pleasure flushed her cheeks. Not knowing how to respond, she looked down at the little boy. "Is that it, Matty? Are we done here?"

The boy shook his head, took another book from the pile on the table and handed it to her.

"No more, Matty," Anne said. "The adults are going to enjoy the blueberry muffins and tea. You can sit here with us or go check to see if the kitties have water. You know that's your job, right?"

Matty looked up at Bay.

She smiled and took the book from him. "How about if we save *County Fair* for next time? Would that be okay?" She flipped the hardback picture over and read the description. "I can't wait to find out why Almanzo is going to the fair."

Matty nodded, took the book from her and added it to his pile. Then he slid off the chair and carried the books out of the kitchen.

David brought his mug and a plate for himself to the table. He chose two fat muffins bursting with blueberries and covered in a crunchy cinnamon and brown sugar streusel, before taking his seat at the head of the rectangular table. "I'm serious, Bay. I can't believe he's taken to you like this. He likes to be read to, but he's very particular about the reader." He held her gaze. "I don't know what you did but thank you."

A little embarrassed, Bay smiled and reached for her cup of tea. "I didn't do anything."

"Well, he was obviously happy to see you." David peeled back the paper from one of his muffins and took a bite. "I hope we see you often."

Bay focused on the muffin that had been sitting on her plate untouched. And thankfully, David began telling them about a pear tree he had managed to graft back in Wisconsin that had survived the trip and was sprouting leaves. Apparently, he'd been on the property all along, but his truck had been parked back behind one of his greenhouses. That conversation led to a discussion about the best pear trees to grow in Delaware, and Anne giving her opinion on which pears made the best pear butter. The next thing Bay knew, she was staring at the clock on the kitchen wall.

"Is the clock right?" she asked, pointing. "Is it that late?"

By then Matty had wandered back into the kitchen. He was playing quietly on the floor with a couple of homemade wood toy trucks. He had filled the beds of them with bits of dry cat food.

David glanced over his shoulder at the clock and back at Bay. "Yup."

Bay jumped to her feet. "I have to go." She took her mug and plate as well as Anne's to the sink. "I didn't mean to stay this long." And truly she hadn't. Two hours? She'd only been there half an hour before David arrived, but the next hour and a half had seemed to evaporate.

Her mother was going to wonder where on earth she had been. Bay had only intended to be gone an hour or so and she'd been gone four.

"Oh my, it is getting late. I suppose I should think about supper. We're just having leftovers," Anne said, getting slowly to her feet. "But I have chores to do before I think about warming things up."

"Thank you so much for the tea and muffin," Bay said as she hurried toward the mudroom to put on her jacket.

David got up from the table, following her. "Glad you stopped by." He stepped into the laundry room and watched her put on her jacket. He lowered his voice. "I'm really looking forward to Thursday."

"Me, too," she said.

"You sure you don't want me to come by your place for you?"

"No need." She carefully took the scarf tied at the nape of her neck and retied beneath her chin without exposing her hair. She'd had no intention of coming here today when she dressed in the morning. She certainly hadn't planned to see David, but she was glad she was wearing one of her nicer everyday dresses and that she'd put on her sneakers that didn't have holes in the toes. "I'll be over after breakfast. That way, I can... see Matty. Maybe read one book."

He laughed and opened the door for her. "I'm glad you came," he repeated, still speaking quietly, his words only for her. "For Matty and Anne's sake, of course, but—" He hesitated. "But I'm glad I got to see you. Thursday seemed like a long way off when we said goodbye the other day."

Bay stepped out onto the porch, unsure what to say. She thought about telling him that she hadn't been able to wait to see him, either, but feeling self-conscious, she offered a quick smile. "See you Thursday." Then she hurried down the steps and across the yard toward the buggy, hoping her mother hadn't noticed how long she'd been gone.

If wishes were horses, Bay thought to herself as, forty-five minutes later, her mother hustled out of the house, meeting her halfway across the porch. "Where have you been, Bay Stutzman? I was worried to death. I was ready to send the boys out to look for your body in a ditch."

"I'm sorry, *Mudder*," she answered, using the more formal word for *mother*. "Time got away from me, is all. I'm fine." She kept the irritation out of her voice. Her mother was right, but it still irked her that her mother kept tabs on her as if she were a child.

"I sent Jesse over to Ginger and Eli's on his scooter two hours ago, looking for you. Ginger thought you were going straight home."

Bay tried to go around her mother, but her mother blocked her escape.

"Where were you?" her *mam* repeated. "Supper's ready to go on the table. If you weren't here by the time we sat down, I was thinking about calling the police." Her face was stern, her eyes practically sparking with anger.

"I'm really sorry," Bay repeated. "It was wrong of me. I should have called and left a message at the harness shop. Of course, I don't know what the chances were you would have gotten my message. Emily isn't getting any better at answering the phone. I don't know why Benjamin keeps letting her do it."

"We're not talking about Emily right now, we're talking about you, *dochter*."

Realizing she wasn't going to get past her mother without an explanation, Bay dropped her hands to her sides. "Remember Anne I told you about? She and her brother helped me with the wagon last week?" She went on without waiting for her mother to reply. "She asked me to stop by sometime. She's recently widowed with a little boy and a baby on the way. She's around my age and she doesn't have any friends who live nearby, and…and she could use a friend. And I like her," Bay added stubbornly.

Her mother crossed her arms over her chest. "That's wonderful that you would be friendly with her. What's her name again?"

"Anne."

Her mother nodded. "I think that's wonderful that you would go to see her, but you should have told me or at least your sister that you were going there."

"But I didn't decide to stop by until after I left Ginger's. It was a nice day for a ride."

"Your impulsiveness will get you into trouble," her mother warned. "I've told you that."

"*Ya*, I know. You're right, and I am sorry. I won't do it again. Next time I go see her, I'll tell you. In fact, I'll be going Thursday. Probably be gone the whole day." She stepped around her mother and darted for the door. "I'll help put supper on the table," she called.

"You know, this is why I'll sleep better at night once you find a husband," her *mam* called after her. "Then he can worry about your coming and goings, and I won't have to!"

Chapter Six

Bay leaned out the passenger-side window of David's truck, as she listened to music on the radio and enjoyed the feel of the wind on her face. The sound of smooth jazz, a kind of music she had never heard before, drifted through the speakers. She was so happy, the happiest she could remember in a very long time. She looked down at Matty, who was sound asleep in his car seat beside her, and she smiled and stroked his silky red hair. Her gaze shifted to David.

He had his window down, too, his arm resting on the door. He was wearing aviator sunglasses, a ball cap that read Clark Seeds, and a chambray shirt and jeans. The puffy vest she was growing accustomed to seeing on him was draped over Matty.

"I had a really good day today," she said.

David pushed a button on the steering wheel and the music got quieter. He looked at her, and she wished she could see his eyes. It was hard to believe she'd only known him a little more than a week. The trip that day to the town of Milton to see the hydroponic greenhouses had seemed to solidify their friendship. Four hours after they left David's place, she felt as if she had known him her whole life. And strangely enough, she felt the same about Matty. Today looking after the little boy, cutting up his chicken fingers at the diner where they ate lunch, and now cuddling him as he slept had felt natural.

"I had a really good day, too, Bay," David said. "I'm so glad you came with me. You had questions I hadn't even thought to ask."

"It was nice of Ronny to be so patient with me and all of my chatter," she said, referring to the owner of the greenhouses. "I didn't mean to be annoying." She studied his handsome face as she spoke. "I was just so fascinated. I would *love* to try growing that way."

"You weren't annoying." He glanced at her, smiling shyly. "I was kind of proud you were there with me, asking so many good questions. You're one smart lady, Bay. Smarter than me. Some of the things Ronny was saying, I'm still processing. I'm ordering those books he recommended. And I'm going to check out the websites."

"I'd love to have a look at the books, when you're done with them." She stared out the window at a field of horses. She was glad David had taken the back roads home. The highway was safe enough in a motor vehicle, but she still preferred the country roads. There was so much to see, and with the land beginning to turn green and blossom with spring, it was a nicer ride. "We don't have internet. Benjamin is trying to convince our bishop that he needs it for the family business, especially now that Joshua and I have the greenhouses and Levi is building buggies. It's so much easier to order over the internet— that's what Levi says, at least. I don't know where he's getting the internet to do it, and I'm not asking."

She chuckled and David chuckled with her. "So your bishop says no on the internet."

She exhaled. "So far, *ya*. He says it will be too hard to keep employees and family off websites. He says if he allows us to order horse liniment one day, the next day someone will be using the computer to stream movies." She laughed again. "I didn't even know what that meant until Joshua told me."

"I can understand both sides," David said

thoughtfully. "There are serious vices that can be gotten online. Plus, it can just be a huge waste of time. And money." He settled both hands on the steering wheel. "We have internet in my office out in the barn, but not in the house. No TV. Anne said that she and Matthew had been discussing getting internet in the house for the business and maybe to stream something family-oriented on Saturday nights, but they never made a decision and then…"

His voice drifted to silence and Bay was quiet for several minutes, letting him deal with the emotion she heard in his voice as he spoke of his brother-in-law's death.

Matty shifted in his car seat between them, but didn't wake, and Bay tucked David's vest tighter around him. "I'm so glad you brought Matty today," she said. "It was a nice surprise. Did he ask to come?"

"You mean did he jump in the truck? Because you know, these days he doesn't ask for anything."

She nodded in understanding. She knew David and Anne were both worried about Matty not talking, but they were trying to trust in the pediatrician's assurances and God's will. "I wondered if he let you know he wanted to come with you or if Anne suggested it."

"Actually, I asked Anne if it was okay if he came with us." His tone sheepish, David took his eyes off the road for a moment to look at her. "I got to thinking, you being a single woman, me a single guy. I didn't know how your parents would feel about me whisking you away in my truck for the day. Or what your bishop would think."

"My parents trust my judgment," she answered carefully. "But I didn't tell them I was going with you today."

"You didn't? Why not?"

She thought on it for a moment before she answered. "I'm not sure. I think because I'm feeling a little hemmed in. By my age, most girls are married and don't have parents keeping an eye on them, telling them what to do and how to do it. Telling them it's time they marry."

"Ah, back to that. Your mother still giving you a hard time?"

"She means well. I know that," Bay told him. "And I know she's trying to understand my perspective. But we're so different. It's hard for both of us."

"Would she be upset if you told her you went with me today? I would never want to cause any problems between you and your family. I really like you, Bay, but if our friendship is a problem, I would understand—"

"It's not a problem," she interrupted. "Meeting you has been the best thing that's happened to me…ever." Surprised by her own words, she sneaked a peek at him to see his reaction.

He looked straight ahead, but he was smiling. "I feel the same way," he told her quietly. He glanced briefly at her and then back at the road. "And I have to admit, I'm a little conflicted because—" He stopped and started again. "Because, well… Well, I'm just going to say it, Bay. If you were Mennonite, I'd ask you on a date."

For a moment, Bay was silent. Stunned. But then she felt a warmth in the pit of her stomach, one that slowly radiated through her body. She had suspected he liked her—but she hadn't quite trusted her own instincts. What did she know about the attraction between a man and a woman? Sure, she had seen her sisters and brothers fall in love and marry but she knew how things looked from the outside were different from how they felt from the inside.

David gripped the steering wheel tightly.

"I shouldn't have said that. Totally inappropriate. I'm so sorry."

"You'd ask me out on a date?" she asked, feeling bold with newfound confidence. She had been right! He *did* like her.

He came to a stop sign at a crossroad somewhere out in the country, west of Milford, and put the truck in Park, giving her his full attention. "I would," he said carefully.

"Well, I'd say yes. If you were Amish," she added quickly. "But I think my mother would have kittens if I came home and told her I wanted to go out with someone who wasn't Amish."

"And I'm not." He took a breath and slowly exhaled, holding her green-eyed gaze. "Is that the end of it?"

Feeling upended, Bay tried to think. Suddenly, she saw so many choices in her life, choices she hadn't contemplated before. "I don't know," she answered honestly. "Do we have to decide right now?"

He shook his head slowly. "We don't."

And then he smiled, and the warmth was there inside Bay again, radiating outward.

Just then, Matty opened his eyes, yawned and looked at her. She smiled down at him and he closed his eyes again.

"You know, that's why I brought Matty

with us today," David went on. "Because I have feelings for you. I know in the church community we grew up in, if you were of marrying age and intended to spend an extended period of time with someone the opposite sex who was also single, we had to have a chaperone."

"I'm glad you brought him along, but it's not necessary. At my age, I don't think my *mam* cares about chaperones." She chuckled. "She just wants me out of the house."

A car approached the intersection behind them. "Aren't you going to go?" she asked David.

With obvious reluctance, he shifted the truck and went through the intersection. "Know how to drive, do you?" he teased.

"No. But I know the same rules apply to a truck as a buggy. You can't sit at stop signs with people behind you."

He laughed as he speeded up. "If you wanted to learn, I could teach you."

"Really?" Bay asked with surprise. "You think I could learn?"

"Bay, I have a feeling you'd be a better driver than I am. Of course you could learn."

She sat back in the seat. Amish weren't supposed to drive, though a bishop occasionally gave a dispensation if a man needed to drive for work. She knew a few young men in Hickory Grove who had learned to drive, some with the bishop's approval, some without. But she didn't know of any women who could drive. The idea of it intrigued her. "Just on your property, right? Not on the road?" she asked.

"Wherever you'd feel the most comfortable."

"I wouldn't want to drive on the road. I'm not really supposed to do that." She flashed him a smile. "But at your place, if I was helping you move stuff in the truck or something, I think I'd like that."

Matty made a sound and Bay saw that he was awake and watching. "Hey, little man," she said. "Have a nice nap?"

The boy nodded and pushed off his uncle's vest.

Bay and David exchanged looks and went back to talking about Ronny's greenhouse setup, and before they knew it, they were back at David's place.

Anne met them in the yard. She had been out collecting eggs in the henhouse and when Bay lifted Matty out of his car seat, he ran into his mother's arms, nearly knocking the egg basket from her hand.

"Oh my," Anne cried, hugging her son.

"Looks like you had a good day." She glanced up at Bay and David getting out of the truck. "Seems like you two had a good time, too," she said, looking from one of them to the other, grinning. "Want to stay for supper, Bay?"

"I'd love to, but I should get home."

David walked around the front of the truck. "How about tomorrow night?" he asked. "That would work, right, Anne? We don't have any plans?"

He held Bay's gaze and she wished she could stay. Because even though they'd been together most of the day, she didn't want to leave David. Not yet. It was a strange feeling for her. She'd never felt this way about a man before. But suddenly, so many things she had heard her sisters say made sense. She was attracted to David.

"Ya," Bay managed before she tore her gaze from him. "I can come tomorrow night."

"Great," Anne said, ushering Matty toward the house.

"Great," David repeated softly, still standing in front of Bay and watching her. "I can't wait."

"We'll eat about six," Anne called over her shoulder, too far away to hear her brother.

"See you at six," Bay repeated to David.

As she stepped onto her push scooter, she calculated how long it would be until she could see him again. Only twenty-two hours! she thought happily.

A month later, Bay carried a chicken, rice and broccoli casserole to Anne's stove and slid it into the oven. "How long does it cook?" She turned to her friend who was sitting at her kitchen table, sipping lemonade Bay had made with the fresh lemons she'd snitched from a big bag at home.

"Forty-five minutes."

"Forty-five minutes," Bay echoed, setting the timer on the stove. Unlike the egg timer they used at her house, this was on the stove and was digital. It was easy enough to use, though, once Anne showed her how.

"Thank you for popping that in." Anne set her glass on the table. "I feel like such a wimp, but I get so tired by this time of day."

"You're not a wimp," Bay insisted, going to the counter to chop the lettuce she'd rinsed off and wrapped in a clean towel to dry.

She knew how to dry it because her mother had taught her, but the chopping was Anne's trick. Bay had never had a chopped salad before she'd eaten it at Anne and David's. It was different from the tossed salads she was used to, but having everything cut into bite-size pieces made it seem wonderfully exotic.

"You're carrying an extra person around with you all day," Bay continued. "And putting the casserole into the oven is the easy part. You did the hard part. Left to me, I'd have made a mess of the recipe, and we'd be having grilled cheese for supper. I'm a terrible cook."

"You're not a terrible cook."

Bay cut her eyes at her.

She and Anne had become good friends. After that first supper Bay had eaten with David, Anne and Matty the day after the trip to Ronny's greenhouses, she had quickly become a regular fixture at the table. She ate with them two or three times a week, depending on her schedule and theirs. If Bay's *mam* thought anything of her spending so much time with Anne's family, or so many missed family dinners, she said nothing. Other than on several occasions, her mother suggested Bay invite them to have supper with her own family.

Bay didn't know why, but she wasn't ready to have David and his family over. Maybe because there was so much commotion with not one but two kitchen tables, three children and a houseful of adults. Not only did her adult siblings Nettie, Tara and Jacob still live at home, but Levi and Eve lived there, too, and there was always someone coming for supper, whether it was Ginger and Eli and their five children, or Lovey and Marshall and their little ones. Or Joshua and Phoebe and their toddler who lived on the property but frequently joined them because Phoebe missed all the tumult now that they were in their own house. Bay told herself it was the chaos she was trying to save David and Anne from, especially considering Anne's condition. Now nearly eight months pregnant, Anne was slowing down and always seemed so tired.

But the truth was that while all those things were true, Bay just wanted to have something of her own. Her friendship with David, Anne and Matty was the one aspect of her life that she didn't have to share with her parents, sisters, brothers, sisters-in-law, brothers-in-law, nieces and nephews. And while Bay loved being a part of a large family, there were days when she didn't want to be a piece of such a large puzzle. She wanted independence.

Seeing the look on Bay's face, Anne began to laugh. "Okay, so you're not the best cook in Kent County, but you're not the worst."

Again, Bay gave her the eye. And then they both laughed.

"You just need practice. And to pay attention to the recipe."

"You mean if it says two cups of cooked noodles, I should add two cups of *cooked* ones, not dry?" She'd made that mistake the week before while trying to help Anne make something called goulash. It hadn't turned into a total disaster, but only because Anne had intervened.

"Exactly." Anne continued to rub her swollen belly. "You're just like David. I write two cans of tomato paste on the grocery list and he brings me two cans of whole tomatoes."

At the mention of David, Bay threw a smile over her shoulder and went back to chopping a carrot for the salad. She and David hadn't spoken again of their attraction to each other since that day in the pickup truck, but she felt like it was an ongoing current continually running between them. She could feel it when she was near him and she could see in his eyes, when they were alone, that he felt it, too.

At first, she had nearly convinced herself it was a passing attraction, at least for her. She'd never liked anyone before and it was exciting. Wasn't it natural that she would feel a light-heartedness whenever they were together? But as the weeks passed, she began to realize that her feelings for David weren't a schoolgirl's infatuation. If she wasn't in love with him, she was falling in love with him. So while she enjoyed every minute she spent with him, whether it was alone in his greenhouse with him, or playing Candyland with him and Matty at the table, she was beginning to worry about where the relationship was going to go.

Of course it couldn't go anywhere. She was Amish. Her parents expected her to marry an Amish man. In fact, the week before, the local matchmaker had stopped by to visit and Bay's *mam* had asked—right in front of her— if Bay was interested in hiring her to find her a husband. Bay had been mortified and angry with her *mam* for embarrassing her, basically suggesting that the reason Bay wasn't married was that she couldn't manage to catch a man.

Bay had politely declined and found an excuse to escape the kitchen. Down at the garden shop, which she and Joshua had finally opened the Wednesday before Mother's Day, she'd taken her frustrations out on seedling trays that needed to be washed and dried. But her mother's suggestion had brought back to the forefront her feelings for David... and where she wanted them to go. Because when she acknowledged her feelings for him, she knew she wanted something more than friendship.

Did Bay want to marry David?

She'd told everyone who would listen that she wasn't ready to marry, so she'd been justifying her frequent visits with David by telling herself she was only seeking his friendship. It wasn't true. But what more could there be? There was no sense in dating because she and David couldn't marry. To marry, one of them would have to leave their church. And David had already left the Old Order Amish, so she would be the one who would have to leave.

Would she be willing to do that to marry David?

The idea had been keeping her up nights, the thought turning over and over in her head. Could she leave her church? What would it mean to her spiritually? And of nearly equal importance, what would it mean to her family? What would living the life of a Mennonite mean to her relationship with her mother and Benjamin? To her sisters and brothers? Sometimes, when a man or a woman who had been baptized left the order, they were shunned by their families. That meant that a person who left the church was no longer welcome at their family's table. Some families even went so far as to no longer speak with the fallen. Bay couldn't see her mother and stepfather doing that, but what if she was wrong?

"That a no?"

Bay spun around, David's voice startling her. He was standing in the doorway between the mudroom and the kitchen, the threshold beyond which muddy boots were not permitted. "I'm sorry." She laughed to cover her embarrassment. She hadn't heard him come in the back door. "Woolgathering again." She covered the salad bowl with its snap-on lid. "Probably why I'm such a terrible cook," she told Anne. Carrying the bowl toward the refrigerator, she said to David, "What's the question?"

"I was wondering, Bay, if you could come down to the greenhouse and help me with something. I'm trying to get some PVC water pipes put together and I need four hands to do it." He held up his hands. "But I've only got two."

Matty popped out from behind his uncle. He was wearing a hoodie sweatshirt and a pair of rubber boots. On the wrong feet, as usual.

"Oh no, little man," Anne warned from the chair. "Boots off. You know better than to track mud through the house."

"Those two hands weren't enough?" Bay asked, her tone teasing. She was thrilled David had come to get her help. He'd decided to set up a small hydroponic growing system on one end of one of his greenhouses, just to see how it went. Bay was fascinated by the whole process and had spent hours reading up on the subject, so much time that Joshua was teasing her about needing to hire another helper to make up for all of the tasks she wasn't getting to in their greenhouse these days.

"He's a good helper, but very short." David whispered the last two words loudly, his hand cupped to his mouth, and everyone laughed.

"I can come. If Anne doesn't need me to do anything else to get supper ready." Bay looked to her friend.

"Go!" Anne shooed. "The both of you. I'm tired of being fussed over."

Matty, who had gone back into the laundry room to get rid of his boots, walked into the kitchen.

"Not going with us, little man?" David asked his nephew.

Bay was so impressed with how good David was with Matty. No father could have been better to the boy, no father kinder and more patient. It was one of the reasons Bay loved...*liked* David so much.

Matty said nothing. Instead, he climbed into his chair and began to dump playdough from containers he'd left on the kitchen table earlier in the day.

David looked to Bay. "Guess that means it's just you and me." She pulled the full apron covered in white daisies over her head and hung it on a hook where Anne kept her aprons. She looked to Anne as she headed for the mudroom. "You need anything else?"

"No, thank you. Go, the both of you," she ordered, feigning impatience.

Bay checked the kitchen clock as she walked into the mudroom. David was waiting at the back door for her now. "I've only got an hour and then I have to head home."

"Not staying for supper?" David asked with obvious disappointment.

She stepped into her sneakers and leaned over to tie them. "Can't. Our bishop and his wife are coming for supper. *Mam* said if I wasn't there, she was going to cut off my ear."

David laughed. "I like her. I can't wait to meet her." He held open the door for Bay.

Outside, they crossed the barnyard. "We may as well take these other pipes down," he said, pointing to his truck loaded with plastic piping.

"Okay."

They were almost to the truck when David turned to her. "Hey, I have an idea. Want to learn to drive?"

Bay stopped. "What?"

"Do you want to learn to drive," he repeated. "You told me you wanted to. We could skip the work and do a little driving."

Before she could respond, he tossed her the keys. She threw out her hand, caught them in midair and smiled hesitantly. "You really think I can learn?"

He laughed and went to get in on the passenger's side. "Are you kidding? I don't think there's anything you *can't* learn to do."

Chapter Seven

David sat back in the passenger's side of his truck, his arm propped across the seat, not quite touching Bay's shoulder, though he wanted to. He watched her as she signaled and made a turn, driving between his first two greenhouses.

Bay was a natural. Like a duck on water.

"How was that?" she asked, glancing at him as she drove down the bumpy gravel lane along the side of his second greenhouse.

David was so proud of her that he couldn't stop smiling. Despite Bay's apprehension, he had known she'd be able to do it. They'd spent the last half hour driving around the farm and she hadn't made a single mistake.

"That was excellent. Except you don't have to signal on private property," he told her with amusement. "In a driveway."

She stuck her tongue at him, then focused on the road again and gave the truck a little more gas.

David laughed. "I told you you'd be able to do this. And not everyone can. Poor Anne hasn't taken well to driving. I keep telling her how much easier her life would be after the baby is born if she could drive. She could leave Matty here with me, and she and the baby could go grocery shopping on their own. She could drive to the church for her ladies' meetings without having to worry about me taking her or catching a ride. I've tried and tried to teach her." He shook his head. "But every time she hits the gas instead of the brake—that's how we got the ding on the front bumper." He pointed to the right front bumper, where there was a small dent from when Anne had hit the milk house. "Or she turns left instead of right. I even took her to a school parking lot when no one was there, thinking it might be easier for her to learn out in the open so she didn't have to worry about hitting outbuildings. It was no use."

"Maybe she needs a little more practice," Bay suggested, trying not to laugh.

David smiled at her. She was such a good soul, always kind, always willing to pitch in to help no matter how hard or boring the work might be. But she could also be fun. The other day Bay had come to help Anne wash all the floors in the house and, over lunch, he had challenged her to a game of checkers. They'd played two games of checkers and then Bay had put Matty on her lap and tried to teach him how to play. When David had gotten up to answer the door, he'd returned to find Matty and Bay sitting across from each other, sliding checkers across the table at each other, knocking one checker into another. Matty had been howling with laughter. Bay was so good with him. She was so patient that, day by day, David could see her drawing the little boy out of the dark cloud he'd been hiding inside since his father's death.

At the end of the sixty-foot greenhouse, Bay braked and came to a gentle stop. "Maybe after the baby is born, her head will be clearer. When Ginger was expecting she said she couldn't add two and two together without getting it wrong, but after Paul was born, her head cleared."

David couldn't take his eyes off Bay's pretty face. She'd been out in the sun and a sprinkling of freckles had appeared across her nose and cheeks. "I don't know," he hemmed. "Anne might be hopeless."

"Nothing and no one is hopeless," Bay told

him firmly. "That's what my *mam* always says." She looked up into the sky at the sun falling on the horizon. "I've already stayed too long. I better get home." She flashed him a smile. "This has been so much fun. I can't thank you enough. Want me to park near the door so you can carry all of the piping inside?" She indicated the greenhouse he planned to use for his hydroponic experiment. He wasn't entirely optimistic he could make it all work, but he wanted to try.

"Nah, I should get inside and help Anne set the table. I'll do it after supper. Now that it's getting warmer, I like to bring Matty outside for a little while after we eat. It wears him out for bedtime and gives Anne time to catch her breath." He pointed in the direction of the barnyard in the distance. "Just take us back to the house."

She nodded but made no move to put the truck in gear again. She just sat there for a moment, looking at him while he looked at her.

David felt a flutter in his chest. One he could no longer deny. For weeks he'd been rationalizing its meaning, but he couldn't do that any longer.

The fact of the matter was, he was falling in love with Bay Stutzman.

And he didn't know what to do about it. His mind told him to keep his mouth shut as he had since the day they made the trip to Sussex County. But his heart…his heart told him he couldn't keep quiet. He wanted to talk to Bay about his feelings for her, if nothing else, then to settle the matter, because obviously this attraction was going nowhere.

Even though he suspected it was mutual.

He could see it in Bay's eyes. He could tell that she had feelings for him. There was a sparkle in her eyes, the faintest smile on her rosy lips. But that day they were driving back from Ronny's greenhouses, they had agreed not to talk about it.

What if she did want to talk about it now, though? That had been a month ago.

But what would be the point?

He'd been asking himself that question for days now.

She was Amish. He wasn't. They were practically Romeo and Juliet material.

But the look in her eyes as she watched him now… His heart fluttered again. Was it too much to hope that maybe they could figure out a way to make a life together? Was it too much to hope that it was what she wanted? He would never ask her to do anything she didn't want to do, certainly not leave her church and the life she had always known. He knew from experience how hard that could be. It still was, sometimes.

But the longer he knew Bay, the more he recognized the restlessness he had felt before leaving his Amish life to become Mennonite. She seemed to question many of the same aspects of Amish ways that he and Anne and their brothers Abe and Hiram had wrestled with, like the often subservient role of women and the belief that education was unnecessary beyond eighth grade.

Was it too much to think that Bay would consider becoming Mennonite to marry him? Just the thought of it nearly made him giddy.

If he and Bay were to marry, they could work together on the farm and run the wholesale nursery business. It was easy to imagine them working side by side each day, laughing and loving every moment of it. It would suit her independent personality. And give her the freedom he sensed she was looking for.

David knew that once she married an Amish man, her domain would go from her greenhouse business to the family home. Her days would be filled not with nurturing plants, but children and her husband. She would be responsible for her own home, the garden, the making of clothing and meals.

And there would be little time for her passion for gardening, once the babies came.

Not that he didn't want children if God so blessed him. But he wanted his wife to be a companion, someone he could work beside each day and share in his daily tasks. He didn't want his marriage to be divided by traditional roles as his parents' had been.

David had no problem with the Amish way of life for others. In some ways, looking back, he knew his life had been simpler when he'd lived without electricity, and shared a bedroom with four brothers. But the path he had chosen as a young man of twenty had been the right one for him. He knew God had meant him to navigate the challenges of moving from the Amish world to the Mennonite one. And he knew now that Kent County, Delaware, was where he was meant to be, here with his sister and Matty…and maybe Bay, too.

There was no way for him to know these things if he didn't explore them, though. And that meant talking about it with Bay. As scary as the idea felt at that moment, he knew he needed to do it. If nothing else, then to know if all of his dreaming was for naught.

"Bay," he said, digging deep to find the courage to say what he wanted to say. "We need to talk. About…us. About what I think is going on here."

In silence, she held his gaze a moment and then looked away. Together they watched a sparrow hawk soar over the field. It flew in lazy circles and then drifted higher until it disappeared.

"*Ya*, I know we need to talk, David," she said quietly. When she looked at him, her eyes glistened with moisture. "But… I'm just not ready. Is that okay?"

He nodded, feeling light-headed. "Of course," he managed. His heart was suddenly pounding in his chest. He hadn't imagined it, this connection he'd been feeling with Bay these last weeks as they'd spent time getting to know each other in his sister's kitchen and in his greenhouses.

Bay settled her hands on the steering wheel, shifted into gear, and this time, she hit the gas pedal with more force. The truck shot forward, and David grabbed the door handle, thankful he was wearing his seat belt.

Grinning, Bay whipped his truck around the back of the last greenhouse and headed for the barnyard. She was only going maybe thirty miles an hour, but it felt like sixty as bits of gravel shot out from under the tires, and the whole truck rocked as it hit the gullies in the lane.

"Whoa!" David cried, laughing. "Easy."

"I've got this!"

She was laughing, too, as they sped between the greenhouses. He couldn't take his eyes off her. She was as beautiful as any woman he had ever known, with her bright red hair, covered mostly with a denim kerchief, little wisps framing her heart-shaped face. And her big green eyes were so expressive he sometimes felt he could read her mind, looking into them.

As they drove into the barnyard, David spotted his sister and Matty coming out of the first greenhouse. Anne was carrying a gathering basket heaped with fresh greens he'd grown and Matty was carrying a handful of parsley as if it were a bouquet.

Bay parked the truck and sat back with a satisfied sigh. "Leave the keys in the ignition?" she asked.

"Sure. I leave them in there all the time on the property." David got out of the truck. "Anne thinks I'm crazy. Says I'm too trusting. That one of these days, I'm going to come outside to find the truck gone."

Bay walked around the front of the vehicle. "I'm going to head home," she called to Anne.

Then to Matty, she raised her hand. "See you another day, little man."

Matty took off across the driveway toward Bay, clutching the parsley.

"You sure you can't stay for supper?" Anne asked, following Matty, but moving far slower than her son. "I'm making a salad with fresh greens David grew to go with the casserole."

Bay dropped her hands to her sides. "Sorry. I can't. I promised my *mam*." She looked down at Matty. "But I'll be back in the next few days." She waved at him. "So it's only bye for now."

Matty looked up at her and waved his free hand. "Bye-bye," he said so softly that for a moment, David thought maybe he'd imagined it.

But he hadn't. Matty had spoken for the first time in six months!

David's breath caught in his throat, and he glanced up at his sister. She looked as shocked as he felt, and he gave a little laugh of joy.

"He's talking," Anne murmured, tears sliding down her cheeks.

Bay grinned and crouched so that she was eye level with Matty. "Bye-bye yourself." She was smiling as hard as David and Anne were. "Can I give you a hug?"

Matty nodded and Bay put her arms around

him and lifted him and spun him around the way David sometimes did. The boy squealed with laugher.

"I'm so happy to hear your voice, Matty," Bay told him. And for the second time that day, David saw her teary-eyed and it touched a place in his heart he hadn't even known existed.

Bay set Matty down, and Anne put her basket on the ground and rushed toward her son. "You talked! See, I knew you could do it. When you were ready," she added, repeating what the pediatrician had told them. She leaned down, one hand on her belly, the other caressing Matty's shoulder. "Can you say *Mama*?"

"Mama," Matty repeated so quietly that his voice barely reached David. But he had heard him.

Matty then pointed at David. "Uncle David." And then he turned to Bay and grinned up at her. "My Bay."

Anne looked up at Bay. "Thank you," she whispered, through her tears. "Thank you so much, Bay."

Bay wiped at her eyes. "No need to thank me. Matty was just taking his time, weren't you?" she said. Then she looked up to meet David's gaze.

"Thank you," he mouthed.

"You're welcome," she mouthed back.

David watched her get on her push scooter and head down the driveway, and he prayed that God would help him find a way to make Bay his wife.

It was almost a week before Bay was able to make it back to David and Anne's. It had been a crazy last few days. There had been one problem after another at the garden shop: the roof had sprung a leak, a stray dog that had gotten inside one of the greenhouses and knocked trays of flowers over, and the credit card system Jacob had convinced Benjamin to invest in had crashed. Then on Saturday, Bay had planned to visit them, but her mother had guilted her into staying home to help whitewash the house in anticipation of hosting church next month.

Hosting church was a big deal because it was usually only once a year. Folks spent months tidying up, painting and even doing landscaping, not for reasons of *hockmut*, a boastful pride, but because it was an honor to host services.

When Bay arrived at David's, she didn't know who was happier to see her: David, Matty or Anne. David waylaid her in the driveway, where they talked for at least half an hour before she made it into the house. The plan was to all go together to Byler's store to do the weekly grocery shopping and have an ice cream cone. However, when she and David went inside, they found Anne was resting on the couch in their living room after having a dizzy spell. Anne decided not to go into Dover but insisted they go without her. Bay and David weren't too happy with the idea of leaving her home alone, but Anne was adamant. And Matty was so excited about the ice cream that, in the end, David wasn't able to say no.

In Byler's store parking lot, Bay got out of the truck and reached in to help Matty from his car seat.

"Need help?" David asked, tucking his keys into his pants pocket as he walked around the front of the truck.

"*Ne*, we've got it." She tickled Matty under the chin. "Don't we?"

Matty giggled and pushed her hand away as she unsnapped the last strap. "Bay," he said and grinned at her.

The sound of his voice saying her name brought up a well of emotions. It was so good to hear his voice, to know that he was going to be okay. Matty still wasn't saying a lot, but, according to David, he was talking more each day. He wasn't participating in conversations yet, but there were a lot of yeses and nos. He also had no problem talking when he wanted something, and he couldn't make his uncle or mother understand. Or they pretended not to understand.

When she turned around with Matty in her arms, David stood right behind them. He took his nephew from her and lowered the boy to the pavement. As he set the boy down between them, David removed his aviator sunglasses and looked into her eyes.

"I've missed you," he said, slipping the glasses into the pocket of his red shirt. He was wearing his Clark Seeds ball cap and jeans with work boots.

Bay felt her face grow warm. "I've missed you, too," she told him, enjoying the connection she felt between them when their gazes met.

And she *had* missed him; she'd been surprised how much. The whole week she'd felt frustrated because she couldn't get away. In retrospect, she realized the week apart had been good for her. It had given her time to examine her feelings for him and determine if she was simply infatuated with the man or if it was more than that. After all, he was the first adult male who had ever paid any attention to her. Sure, once in a while, a boy would try to talk to her at church or when he stopped by the greenhouse to buy flowers for his *mam*, but they rarely ever said more than a hello the second time they saw her. Bay always felt like she made men her own age uncomfortable—Amish men, at least.

But not David.

She stood there for a moment, looking into his eyes, enjoying the warmth of the sun on her face and the warmth of his gaze. She hadn't imagined her attraction to him nor his attraction to her. She had accepted that fact sometime over the last week. Then moved onto the next question.

Was she interested in seeing where the attraction led them?

Was she interested in pursuing marriage? She had been raised to believe that dating was only for a couple seriously considering marriage, and while she would not judge others, it was the only option for her. She wasn't interested in casual dating. If she did feel strongly for David, if she loved him, was she willing to leave her Amish faith to be his wife?

Bay had been asking herself that for days and she still wasn't sure of the answer. It was too much to wrap her head around it. But after sifting through her feelings for David, she was pretty sure she was in love with him. Which meant it was time they had the talk she'd been avoiding.

Suddenly, Matty darted out from between her and David, and David took off after his nephew.

"Matty, you know the rules," David admonished as he caught up to the boy and took the child's hand in his bigger one. "You have to hold an adult's hand in parking lots."

"Horse!" Matty said, pointing.

There was a small painted pony tied up at the hitching post near the side of the store. Bay recognized the pony at once. Chester belonged to Eunice Gruber's mother, who had recently moved in with Eunice and her family. Bay and her family had belonged to the same church district as the Grubers until recently, when the church divided because of so many new families moving into the area.

Bay glanced around, hoping Eunice hadn't come with her mother to Byler's. Bay liked Eunice, but she was a busybody and a gossip. If Eunice saw Bay there with David, it wouldn't be long before she was at Bay's *mam's* table tattling. And that would be a disaster.

Bay scanned the parking area for the older

woman and saw nothing but cars and pickups in the larger lot, and then the pony and
cart and one horse and black buggy tied up
on the side of the building. There were a few
Englishers in the parking lot, some pushing
carts out of the store while others walked inside, but she didn't see any Amish.

"Come on, Matty." David tugged at his
hand. "Let's get inside and get our groceries. I thought we'd have our ice cream in the
truck on the way home." He looked over his
shoulder at Bay. "If that's okay with you. I'm
concerned about Anne. If she's not feeling
better by the time we get home, I'm going to
insist she call her doctor."

"That's fine," Bay agreed. She was worried about Anne, too. She hadn't looked good
to her when she arrived. Anne's face had a
gray cast.

Bay scanned the parking lot again for her
nosy neighbor, wondering if she should have
stayed at the house with Anne. Bay realized
now that she hadn't thought about the possible consequences of going out in public with
David.

Her mother would be hurt if someone else
told her first that Bay was seeing a man. An
Englisher. Not that David was exactly an *Englisher*, but no matter what he was, Bay knew

her mother would want to hear the information from her daughter and not a neighbor. And Bay knew it was time she told her *mam*. She was feeling guilty that she hadn't said anything already. She'd been waiting for the opportunity, or would be, once she figured out exactly what she was going to say.

"Horse," Matty repeated, stamping his foot. He was wearing new green Crocs on his bare feet. The weather had turned from spring to summer over the weekend, and it was in the high seventies that day. Bay hadn't even needed a sweater when she'd ridden over to David's on her push scooter.

"See horse," Matty told David emphatically.

David sighed, and Bay knew he would give in. Matty had asked with words. How could David deny him?

"Can I get a *please*, little man?" David asked.

Matty looked up, the cutest smile on his face. *"Pwease,"* he said clearly and loudly.

Bay laughed and shrugged. "He said *please*."

David exhaled and tugged on the brim of his ball cap. "Fine. But just a quick pet, and then we have to get our groceries and get home to your mama. Okay?"

Matty nodded.

So they went over to see the pony, and while Matty petted him, Bay kept watching over her shoulder for Eunice. What she was going to do if she spotted the older woman, she wasn't sure, but she still kept an eye out for her.

"Looking for someone?" David asked.

She turned back quickly. "What? No… um… *Ya*, I know the lady who owns the pony and cart. She lives in Hickory Grove."

David crossed his arms over his chest as Matty continued to stroke the pony. "Ah." There was curiosity in his tone. He could tell that she wasn't going to be excited if she did spot Eunice.

Bay thought about changing the subject, but if she truly wanted to consider something beyond friendship with David, she knew she could never deceive him in any way. She pressed her lips together. "My family doesn't know," she said, feeling ashamed as she admitted it aloud.

His forehead creased. "Doesn't know what?"

Bay met David's gaze. "My mother, Benjamin, my brothers and sisters. They don't know about you. They think I come to your place to visit Anne."

He was quiet for a minute, then pushed his sunglasses up on his head and rubbed his eyes with his finger and thumb. "So you've been leaving me out of the conversations?"

She nodded.

"Can I ask why, though I've got a pretty good guess."

Bay watched Matty move from the pony to the cart. He was checking out the wooden wheels. She made herself look at David again. "Because I like you. A lot. And I'm afraid," she admitted, struggling to keep emotion out of her voice.

He seemed to hold his breath for a moment. "You're afraid that if you tell your parents you're dating a Mennonite man, they'll forbid you. Because you know, Bay, that's sort of what we've been doing for weeks. Maybe not in a conventional way, but—" He tilted his head from side to side. "We're both pretending it's something else, but it's not."

He surprised her by taking her hand. It wasn't that they had never touched before. They touched when passing things to each other in the greenhouse as they worked on his hydroponic system. They touched when they passed Matty back and forth or when Bay gave David the mama cat in the house to take outside. But this touch was different. It was more personal. It made her heart pound in her chest and she wanted him to hold her hand forever.

She was in love and she couldn't deny it any longer.

"Is that why you're afraid? Because you think your mother and stepfather will tell you that you can't see me anymore?" David pressed.

"Not Benjamin. He'll stay out of it. And I don't think *Mam* will outright forbid me. She's always said that forbidding someone to do something is an invitation to do it." She paused and then went on. "But she's going to be very upset with me. Disappointed with me."

David didn't take his gaze from hers but he let go of her hand. "Bay, you have to tell her."

"I know," she murmured. Her hands felt sweaty and she wiped them on her apron. "I realized today that I can't put it off any longer."

David looked away. "Matty, don't get inside the cart," he warned. "It isn't ours. One more minute, and then we go inside, okay?" He returned his attention to Bay. "Will you tell her today when you get home?"

She chewed on her lower lip. "I'll try."

He smiled. "I doubt it will be as bad as you think. From what you've told me about your mother, she loves you and only wants what's best for you. Worrying about this sort of thing is always worse than actually doing it."

"You're right." She lifted her hands and let them fall. "I just need to do it and get it over with."

"And what will you tell her?"

She looked up at him through her lashes. "That…that I really like you and—" She pressed her lips together. "That you like me and that's all I know right now. But that I want to keep seeing you."

"And I want to keep seeing you. You know that, right?" he asked.

She nodded.

David was quiet for a moment, then went on. "And I hope that you realize that my intentions are honorable. I know this is more complicated for you than for me, but—" He stopped and started again. "But we'll figure it out, Bay, once we talk about what we both want. I think we need to make time for that talk."

"*Ya,* we do." Bay sniffed and used the corner of her white apron to wipe her eyes. She was embarrassed that she was tearing up, but she couldn't help it. She'd never felt so emotional before. David made her feel this way. Because she wanted to be with him. She wanted to be with him always.

"Well," David said slowly. "I'm glad you're ready, because I'm past ready. And Anne is always on me, telling me we need to do it sooner rather than later."

Bay cringed. "Anne knows?"

He laughed. "She says it's pretty obvious. And she adores you. She has this idea that you and I would make a couple." His tone had lightened. "So let's set some time aside."

She nodded, wishing she could feel his hand on hers again.

"But right now, here, is obviously not the place. And not with little ears nearby." He cocked his head in Matty's direction. "Let's go shopping and get home to check on Anne. Maybe you can come over tomorrow or the next day and we can sit down together alone."

"I can't come tomorrow. Joshua has a dentist appointment and I have to run the shop. Maybe Wednesday." She grimaced. "No, we're meeting with someone about buying flowers from us wholesale on Wednesday. Maybe Thursday?" she said hopefully.

"Let me know what day works for you. I can do it anytime. Maybe we can go for a ride in the truck, just you and me." She was looking into her eyes again. "Get a bite to eat.

There's this food truck in Clayton that everyone has been saying is amazing."

She smiled shyly, not feeling quite herself, but more alive than she'd ever felt before. Suddenly, she could see a whole life in front of her with David. They could run his greenhouses together. And while she would no longer attend the Amish church, she could attend Mennonite services. Just as David and Anne did now. "I'd like that."

He held her gaze a moment longer, a moment she wanted to go on forever but then he looked to Matty.

"Ready to go inside, little man?" he called, putting out his hand to his nephew.

"Ice cream!" Matty cried happily and ran to take David's hand.

Together, the three of them set off down the sidewalk. As they walked through the automatic doors and into the store, Bay wondered which looming conversation she was more nervous about, the one with her mother or David. Because one or both might change her life forever.

Chapter Eight

A few days later, David stood in the middle of the kitchen, frowning at his sister. She stood in front of him, her arms crossed over her chest. She looked tired. Her skin wasn't the usual rosy color, and she had dark circles under her eyes. And she was angry with him for *fussing* over her.

"I'm not fussing," he defended.

He was, but only because he was worried about her. The baby was due in five weeks. Wasn't it time she started taking it easy? This little spat between them had begun when he'd innocently asked her what she thought about hiring someone to help her with the cleaning and gardening once the baby was born.

"You *are* fussing. It's like you think you're my *grossmama*," Anne sputtered. "There's nothing wrong with me. I'm not sick. I'm having a baby, which is the most natural thing in the world. I know what I'm doing." She pointed a finger at him the way their mother used to. "I've done it before, you know."

David eyed Matty, who was sitting quietly in the doorway between the kitchen and hall, playing with a new green tractor and wagon he'd bought for him. The boy didn't seem to be paying any attention to them. Sadly, he was probably used to his mother and uncle's squabbles. They were happening with increasing frequency and always over the same subject.

"I'm just trying to be helpful," David told his sister, taking his voice down a notch.

"That's nice, but don't," Anne snapped back, obviously frustrated with him. She raised her hand in a stop motion. "Just don't."

He watched her turn away and go to the kitchen counter where she took out a mixing bowl and measuring cups from the cabinet above. "And stop being cranky with me," she tossed over her shoulder.

He opened his arms. "I'm not."

"You are. You haven't been yourself since you and Bay and Matty went to Byler's at the beginning of the week. Did you and Bay have a disagreement?" She walked to the refrigerator and pulled out a carton of eggs and a stick of butter. "Is that why she hasn't been here? Please don't tell me you've argued with her because if you chased her off—"

"We didn't argue," he interrupted.

Anne was really trying his patience now. Maybe because somewhere in the back of his mind, he was beginning to wonder if he *had* chased her off with his insistence it was time she told her mother about him. And time he and Bay discussed their relationship and where it was going.

"Bay's been busy," David said. "Yesterday we were supposed to go get lunch at that food truck I was telling you about, but she had to cancel. Something about her mother needing her. They're hosting church this summer and you remember what that's like."

Anne carried the eggs and butter to the counter. "Was it supposed to be a date?" Her tone had gone from one of irritation to concern.

David thought about it for a moment. "We were going to go for a ride, get something to eat, and talk. Like have *a talk*."

"About your future?" Anne asked.

He nodded.

"Good. I know it's probably harder for Bay than for you, but you need to discuss how you feel about each other so you can decide what's to be done. Have you told her you love her?" She went on without taking a breath. "Because that makes a difference to a woman. We need to hear the words, not just see the actions. But maybe that's true for men, too," she mused.

Did he tell Bay he loved her? Anne's question so surprised him that he barely heard what else she said. "I…haven't—" he sputtered. "I'm not—"

"You're not what?" she asked, peeling a ripe banana and dropping it into a bowl. "You're not in love with her? You most certainly are, and I suspect she's in love with you." Picking up a potato masher, Anne turned around, giving him a look he recognized as she shook the kitchen tool at him. Their mother had made the same face when challenging him. "There's no question. You both love each other, and she'd be a good wife to you, and I think you'd be a good husband to her. But there's that one *tiny* problem."

He exhaled loudly. "Right. Just a tiny problem. She's Amish, and I'm not." He frowned. "She hasn't told her parents anything about me. They don't know I exist, and that concerns me." He rocked his head from side to side. "Well, they know I helped her that day of the accident, but they think she's been coming here to see you."

Anne turned around, wiping her hand on her apron. "Oh dear."

"Yeah, and it worries me. Even though we haven't talked about it yet, obviously, the only thing that could be done if we are serious about each other would be for Bay to become Mennonite." He met her gaze, his heart feeling heavy. "I can't go back, Anne. Not even for Bay. If I did, I wouldn't be true to myself."

She offered a generous smile. "I know. But she knows that, too. Bay and I have talked about why I left the Amish way of life. Why you did. She said she's had some of the same feelings lately about her life. Like maybe she's been trying to make herself fit in when the fact of the matter is, it doesn't fit her."

"Really?" He'd had no idea that Anne and Bay had discussed the matter. "Why didn't you tell me?"

She added another banana to the bowl and began to mash it. "Because girl talk is not something meant to be shared with others."

"Not even me?" he asked. "I'm your brother."

"Not even you," she said as she added another soft banana to the bowl. "We didn't talk specifically about her leaving the church to marry you. We both kind of danced around the subject, but she knew that's what we were talking about."

He thought for a moment and then said, "Wow. And I was afraid she wasn't that interested in me. Or at least in marrying me." There it was. He'd said it out loud. He wanted to marry Bay.

She turned to him again. "What would make you think she wasn't interested in you?"

"I don't know. Maybe the fact that she's been sneaking behind her family's back, coming here. Don't you find that concerning? Her mother knows nothing about me, and her mother is the one pushing her to find a husband."

"Ah, that." Anne set the masher in the sink.

"Ah, that?" He raised an eyebrow. "I'm afraid that maybe I'm just, I don't know, a flirtation."

"A flirtation?" Anne laughed. "Maybe you don't know her as well as you think you do. Bay is not that kind of woman. Even though she may not feel like she fits into her world anymore, she still carries a lot of Amish beliefs. She'd never toy with your emotions, David."

"Then why hasn't she told her mother about me?"

"You forget how complicated it is. Leaving the life." She narrowed her gaze. "How long did you wrestle with the idea of leaving the church before you said a word even to me?"

David thought back to that time. He'd only been nineteen when he had realized he would never be the man he was meant to be if he remained Amish. Anne had been the first person he had taken into his confidence when he began considering leaving. "Months," he answered. "Maybe a year."

"Exactly. And once Bay tells her family she cares for you, she's made a declaration. They'll know that having left the Amish church, you have no intention of becoming Amish again. Even if that would be allowed, which is highly doubtful. Which means," she said slowly, "they'll know that she's considering leaving."

"You really think she is?" Hope fluttered in his chest. To leave the church for him would be a huge sacrifice for Bay. Would she do it? Every time he got his hopes up, he tried to temper them with logic, but it was becoming more difficult with each passing day.

Anne leaned against the kitchen cabinet, stroking her abdomen. "Why do you think she's been coming here all this time? Not in the hopes you'll run her off the road again."

"I did not run her off the road!"

Anne chuckled. "You know what I mean. She's coming here to see you. To be with you, David."

"But she really likes you. And Matty, too."

"I know she likes us. But she's fallen in love with you."

Even though David knew in his heart of hearts that he had fallen for Bay, he still found it hard to believe that a woman like her could be interested in a guy like him. She was so perfect and he wasn't. "So you don't think she hasn't told her parents about me because I'm just a passing fancy."

She laughed. "Bay hasn't told them because once she does, you know what's going to happen. The bishop will be called in, and the preachers will be at the house. Everyone in the community will band together to convince her that our life as Mennonites is not the life for her. They'll try to persuade her that you're not the man for her."

"Her brother Levi is one of her preachers."

"That's even worse. Can you imagine sitting at the table three times a day with him?" She turned back to the counter and opened the egg carton. "Oh no."

"What?" David asked.

She held up two eggs. "I'm one short." She

sighed. "I sold my last dozen this morning to Mae Driskel, and I didn't collect the eggs yet. I didn't have it in me," she admitted.

"What are you making?" David asked.

"Banana bread."

His eyes lit up. "With chocolate chips?"

"I could be persuaded to add chocolate chips. And some maraschino cherries," Anne said, "if you'd be willing to collect the eggs."

David looked to Matty, who had filled his toy tractor's wagon full of pink plastic piglets. "Hear that, Matty? Mama needs eggs so she can make us banana bread." He widened his eyes excitedly. "Should we go get eggs in the henhouse?"

"Get eggs for Mama!" Matty leaped to his feet.

David raised his brows at Annie, and they both laughed as Matty grabbed his hand and began pulling him in the direction of the back door.

Twenty minutes later, David and Matty walked onto the back porch with a basketful of eggs. As David opened the back door, Matty spotted a line of ants on the edge of the step and crouched down in fascination to watch them.

"Bugs," Matty declared, pointing.

"Ants," David said. "Look at them all. Let

me take these eggs into your mama, and then when I come back out, we'll see where those little guys are going. I think they're probably carrying some kind of food to their nest. Be right back. Stay on the porch, okay?"

Matty nodded, his eyes round with enthusiasm over his discovery.

David walked into the mudroom, letting the screen door close behind him. The hinges were squeaking, and he made a mental note to get out the WD-40 and lubricate them. "You're not going to believe how many eggs Matty and I found," he called to his sister. "Did you forget to collect—"

He halted just inside the kitchen and stared for a moment, trying to comprehend what he was seeing. Surely this was a bad dream. Surely—"Anne!" He raced toward her, the egg basket still in his hand. "Anne!"

His sister lay unconscious on her side, on the floor.

David dropped to his knees, the eggs rolling out of the basket as it tipped when he set it down on the floor. "No, no," he muttered, rolling his sister on to her back and touching her face. "Anne!" She was still breathing, but he didn't know what was wrong with her. She wouldn't wake up. "Anne! Please!" But she still didn't respond.

David yanked his cell phone from his back pocket and hit buttons.

A young woman spoke. "911, what's your emergency?"

Bay glanced at the clock on her mother's kitchen wall as she set a big basket of potatoes down next to a bin of onions on the floor. It was two o'clock and it would take her and Ginger at least another hour to finish cleaning out the pantry. This meant there was no way she would make it to David's today, either. And she'd already had to cancel the day before because instead of the 500 six-inch plastic pots suitable for geraniums that she'd ordered, she'd received 1000 three-inch pots. She'd had to arrange to have the delivery returned and the correct order sent again. When she spoke briefly with David on the phone from the harness shop, they agreed that their lunch date could be postponed. But he was as eager to talk as she was, and they had hoped she could come by this afternoon and go for a walk. There were trails in the woods on the back of his property he wanted to show her, anyway. But today wouldn't work, either.

"Why did *Mam* ask you to come over today to clean her pantry?" Bay questioned Ginger as she walked back in, trying not to sound too grumpy. "Doesn't she know you have enough to do in your own home?"

Ginger was busy washing off the floor-to-ceiling wooden shelves with a soapy rag. "She didn't ask me to clean out the pantry. I volunteered. You know how she can get worked up when it's her turn to host church. She pretends she isn't, but she is." She shrugged, dipped the rag into the water and wrung it out. "And I want to help. Remember how much time she spent helping me last winter when Eli and I were hosting? She scrubbed the grout in my bathroom, for goodness' sake."

Bay unfolded the step stool and climbed up to grab a tray of canned goods. "But you were a newlywed with four children and still carrying that one under your apron," she argued, pointing to baby Paul asleep in an infant seat in the middle of one of the kitchen tables.

"I like helping," Ginger said firmly. "And with Eli taking the boys to work with him today, it was a perfect opportunity for Lizzy and Paul and me to spend the day here. I like cleaning. I find a clean kitchen or closet or drawer very satisfying. And when *Mam* said she was going to get you to help with the pantry, I offered to help because I wanted to see you. I love my new life with Eli and the children, but I miss you, *Schweschder*."

Bay exhaled impatiently as she carried the tray out to the table, setting it down carefully so as not to disturb her sleeping nephew. "I'm sorry. I don't mean to be cranky." She turned around to face Ginger. "It's just that I don't have time for all of this. Things have been crazy at the garden shop and—" A lump rose in her throat and she swallowed hard, suddenly fighting tears. What was wrong with her? She rarely cried, and when she did, it wasn't over something so trivial as a mistake in an order.

Ginger walked into the kitchen. "What's wrong?"

"Nothing," Bay argued, shaking her head. "I just…" Tears welled in her eyes, and she realized she needed to talk to someone. "I haven't told *Mam* about David," she blurted. "And he says I need to. And we were supposed to get together this week to talk about our relationship, but I've been too busy, and—" She raised her hands and let them fall. "And I… I think I'm in love with him, but I'm afraid to tell *Mam* and Benjamin because—" Her voice caught in her throat, and she couldn't finish.

"Oh, *Schweschder.*" Ginger took Bay's trembling hand between her own and peered into her face. "You're afraid because marrying David would mean leaving your life here to begin a new one with him," she said. "It would mean leaving our church."

Bay nodded, breathing deeply.

Ginger hugged her. "It's going to be all right."

"I know." Bay sniffed, clinging to her sister. She paused for a moment to catch her breath and stepped back. "I know I need to tell *Mam*. I keep trying to find the chance, but she and I haven't seen eye to eye lately and she's so worked up about hosting church and—"

"You have to tell her, Bay," Ginger said gently. "For your own piece of mind. And David's."

"But she's going to be so angry."

The baby began to fuss, and Ginger reached out and touched his infant seat. The seat began to bounce ever so gently, soothing Paul, and he went back to sleep. Bay was fascinated that her sister reacted so calmly to the child's cries and wondered if that came naturally when one had a baby or if it was learned. She didn't feel as if she had any natural mothering instincts, but if she and David had children of their own, would she learn to be the kind of mother Ginger was?

"Bay," Ginger said. "*Mam's* not going to

be angry with you. She might even be able to help you figure out what you truly want to do."

Feeling flushed, Bay pressed her hand to her forehead. "I know. You're right." She met her sister's gaze. "But you know how she can be. She always thinks she knows what's best for me. She doesn't listen to me. She doesn't understand me. I don't think she really sees me for who I am."

"I don't know about any of that, but I can tell you, even though I'm new at this mothering, I would do anything to be sure our children feel comfortable in their own skin." Ginger's eyes suddenly grew moist. "Even let them go to the *Englisher* world if that was what was right for them. If that was where God called them."

Bay gave her a wry smile. "If I married David—and I'm not saying I'm going to—but if I did, I wouldn't exactly be joining the world of the English. David and Anne live much the way we do. God is still the center of their life. They just have electricity and a truck."

The back door opened, and Bay and Ginger looked at each other and, without speaking, moved into the pantry to return to what they were doing. Just in case it was their mother.

She had gone down to the harness shop to speak to Benjamin about whether or not the chicken coop needed a fresh coat of paint.

Ginger picked up the wet rag and began to scrub a shelf.

Bay climbed the step stool again to be sure she'd not left anything on the top shelf that was out of sight. "If you hand me the rag, I'll wipe this shelf down," she told her sister.

"Bay." Their mother walked into the kitchen. Her cheeks were rosy, and she was slightly out of breath. "My goodness," she said, pressing her hand to her chest. "I don't know what made me think a woman my age ought to be walking that fast." She met Bay's gaze. "Phone call for you at the shop. Your friend Anne's brother." Her face softened. "He said it's urgent."

The words were barely out of her mother's mouth before Bay was off the step stool and running through the kitchen. She flew out the back door, across the porch and into the lane. It seemed like it took forever for her to make it all the way to the harness shop. The last steps between the shop door and the phone on the far side of the cash register counter seemed to take the longest.

She grabbed the cordless phone lying on the counter. "David?" she said, out of breath.

"Bay." His voice was barely recognizable. "I need you. Can you come?"

"Of course. To the house?" She gripped the phone. "What's happened?"

"Not the house," he said, speaking fast. "The hospital. Anne collapsed. She was unconscious when I found her. I called 911, and they took her by ambulance. I don't know what's wrong with her. She was awake by the time I got here, but they only let me see her for a second. I'm still waiting for the doctor to tell me what's going on."

Bay felt as if she couldn't breathe for a second. *Not her Anne.* "I'm coming. I'll be there just as fast as I can. Is Matty with you?"

"Um…no." He sounded disoriented. "A friend from church picked him up. I have no idea how long we'll be here, and I didn't want him to get scared. I'm not sure it was the right thing to do. Anne might be upset with me, but…"

"No, no. You did the right thing. I'm sure Anne will agree. I'm coming now. Is there anything you need me to bring you?"

"No. I'll either be in the waiting room of the emergency department or in the back with her."

"Don't worry, I'll find you," Bay said. "I'll be right there, David. All right?"

"All right," he repeated, his voice breathy. "Bay?"

"Yes?"

"Pray for her."

The tone of his voice scared her. This was serious. "I will, David."

The phone disconnected, and Bay stood there for a moment, frozen in fear for Anne and her baby. For Matty and for David. But then she pushed her emotions aside and moved into action. From the bulletin board behind the register, she grabbed the list of *English* drivers they used when a horse and buggy wasn't ideal. She called the first phone number on the list. If no one answered, she'd call the next one and the next one. She'd call a dozen if she had to until she found someone who could get her quickly to the hospital.

She got a recording at the first number, hung up, and dialed the second. As it rang, she heard the bell over the door jingle, and she saw her mother. Again, Bay got a recording and hung up.

"How is your friend?" her mother asked, genuine concern on her face.

"I don't know," Bay said, flustered. "Not good. She's due in five or six weeks and David—her brother," she added, "found her unconscious. She was taken to the hospital by ambulance. I'm trying to find a driver, so I can get there. To be with her. She must be so scared."

"Here. Give me the phone." Her mother put out her hand. "I'll make the calls. You run up to the house and get ready to go. I'll get you a driver."

"You will?" Bay felt as disoriented as David had sounded.

Her mother took the cordless phone from her. "I'll call Lucy. She's not as busy as some of the others. Some don't like her attitude."

Bay's mother walked around the counter as Emily, Benjamin's new hire, came out of the back. "I thought Jesse was covering me for my break."

Bay's mother gave her one of her looks. "I'm not here to run the cash register, dear. I'm making a call."

Emily looked to Bay.

"And she isn't here to cover you for your break, either." Bay's *mam* pointed to the door. "Go," she mouthed to Bay and then into the phone, she said, "Lucy, glad I caught you. It's Rosemary Miller in Hickory Grove. One of my daughters needs a ride to the hospital. No, she's fine. A friend, but it is an emergency. Can you come for her now?"

As her mother made the arrangements, Bay hurried out of the shop, eager to get to Anne. And to be there for David.

Chapter Nine

Bay and David sat side by side in Anne's hospital room, talking quietly while she slept. In the background, there was the sound of two heart monitors beeping steadily: Anne's and the baby's. When Bay had arrived at the hospital, David was still sitting nervously in the emergency department waiting room. A few minutes later, a nurse called them back to see Anne and speak with the doctor. The nurse must have assumed Bay was either Anne's sister or David's wife, because, before seeing Anne, they were both ushered to a small office where Anne's midwife and an obstetrician from her office met with them.

Anne had been diagnosed with peripartum cardiomyopathy, a dangerous and rare type of heart failure. Anne's midwife, Julie, explained that it could develop during pregnancy or right after delivery and was a condition that weakened the heart muscle. The weakened heart would become enlarged, and blood wasn't pumped properly to the rest of her body. The diagnosis explained Anne's increasing tiredness that went beyond the usual fatigue of the last trimester of pregnancy. It also explained other symptoms she'd kept from David and Bay, like feeling out of breath at times and severe swelling of her hands and feet. The condition was likely also the explanation for the dark circles that had appeared under her eyes recently.

After the condition was explained to David and Bay, they, Julie and the doctor joined Anne in her hospital room. Together, they went over the diagnosis and a treatment plan. Through the whole process David listened and nodded, but it was Bay and Anne who asked questions. Anne's first question was: Had she done anything to cause the heart condition? She had not. Bay asked if her condition would right itself once the baby was born. It would not, they were told, as her heart had already been damaged.

Anne was now being treated with several medications, and she and the baby were safe for the moment. However, the doctor explained, her tone grave, that if there wasn't improvement, the baby would need to be delivered by cesarean section within the next twenty-four hours. Otherwise, Anne would remain in the hospital on bed rest until she went into labor naturally.

Bay had been surprised by how calmly Anne had taken the diagnosis. There were no hysterics, no tears. Once the doctor and midwife left, Bay sat down on the edge of Anne's bed, took her hand, and asked her how she was doing, considering all that had been said. Anne had calmly declared that God's will would be done and that she was certain her and Matthew's second child would be born safely into the world. She insisted that they all needed to pray for her and the baby.

Once all of the commotion of Anne's admission to the hospital had quieted, Bay had offered to sit in the waiting room so Anne could rest. She had no intention of leaving David alone in the hospital, but she wanted to give them some privacy. Though David appeared to be taking the whole situation calmly, Bay knew he was a mess. She could see it in his eyes. And Bay suspected Anne could see it, too, because when David stepped out to get some ice, Anne had asked Bay to vow she would look after her brother and her son until she and the baby were home safely. Bay held her friend's hand and made that promise.

Bay and David had been together most of the day, and she didn't know whether it was the physical proximity or Anne's illness, but in the last hours, Bay felt their relationship had moved from one phase to another. They hadn't talked about what they were going to do about their feelings for each other. It didn't seem appropriate with Anne right there, even though she had slept most of the day. However, David and Bay were acutely aware of the undercurrent of emotion rippling between them.

"She looks better," David observed quietly. He looked to Bay. "Doesn't she? There's some color in her cheeks now. Maybe she just needed some rest. Maybe her heart's not as bad as the cardiologist thinks."

An hour ago, Anne's new cardiologist had stopped by to check on her. The woman was not as warm and personable as Julie, nor the obstetrician, but as Anne had pointed out when the doctor left, she wasn't looking for a best friend. She needed a doctor who could treat her medically.

"David," Bay said gently. "We've talked to three medical professionals today. They all gave the same diagnosis, and you saw the echocardiogram. It was easy to see what the cardiologist was talking about when she showed us what Anne's heart looked like and then the picture of what Anne's heart *should* look like."

Bay had never heard of an echocardiogram before that day, but she'd read all of the literature the cardiologist had provided. She then explained it all to David when he said he was too antsy to read through the pile of papers on Anne's nightstand.

"I can't believe this is happening." David took a deep breath and exhaled. "But it sounded like the medicine might help, right?" His eyes sought hers. "The cardiologist said the combination of medicines would keep her from going into heart failure."

The cardiologist had actually said that she was hopeful the drugs would prevent heart failure. Bay had read between the lines and understood that Anne's condition was grave, maybe graver than David understood, but she didn't know that it would help to explain that to him right now.

"I think we need to give the medicine time," Bay told David. He looked exhausted. "When did you last eat?" she asked.

"I had those peanut butter crackers a while ago," he reminded her. He had gotten a pack from a vending machine, and they'd shared them. Anne wasn't allowed to have anything to eat in case she had to have an emergency C-section.

Bay frowned. "I mean real food. Breakfast, I would guess."

He nodded. "Anne made us creamed beef and buttermilk biscuits. She knows Matty and I love fresh biscuits with our breakfast."

"I think you need to get something to eat," Bay told him. "Why don't you go down to the cafeteria? When my *mam* had foot surgery, Ginger and I ate there a couple of times. They have soups and salads and sandwiches and usually a hot dish like spaghetti. I was surprised how good it was."

David worked his hands. "I don't know. You think it's okay to leave her?"

"It'll be fine," Bay insisted. "She told us she didn't need us to sit here all day."

His gaze shifted to the monitors on both sides of the bed. "I don't know if I *can* leave her."

"Sure you can. I'll stay here with her. You need to keep up your strength, David. You're going to have your hands full when she and the baby come home."

He seemed to chew over the idea of that for a moment. "I guess you're right."

Bay kept her tone upbeat even though she was just as concerned about Anne and the baby as David was. "When you go to the cafeteria, you can call and check in on how Matty is doing. Take a little walk, maybe. It will be good for you to stretch your legs."

"I have to call Rich from church." David ran his fingers through his red hair. "He left me a phone message. He offered to take care of the animals, so I don't have to worry about getting home for feeding time. Anne said I should let him do it. That you have to let people help you."

"My *mam* always says that gifts have to work in both directions. That you can't do things for others but never be willing to accept others' help."

David smiled. "I'm going to like your mother. She seems like a wise woman."

"She says she's wise only because of all the mistakes she's made in her life," Bay said with a chuckle. "Now go on. Go get something to eat. I'll be right here when you get back."

David met her gaze again and then surprised her by taking her hand.

Bay glanced at Anne, but she was still asleep.

"Is this okay?" David asked, quietly. "I don't want to make you feel uncomfortable."

They both looked at their hands intertwined on the arm of her chair, and Bay realized how right it seemed, holding hands this way. His warm hand, bigger than hers and a little rougher, felt good. It felt comforting and, at the same time, sent shivers of warmth through her body.

"*Ya*, this is nice," she murmured.

He squeezed her hand. "I've wanted to do this for weeks. I've just been trying to get up the nerve to do it."

He hesitated and then went on. And even though they were in a hospital room with monitors beeping inside and outside the room and there were hushed voices and footfalls in the hallway, Bay felt like there was no one in the world but the two of them.

"I didn't know if holding hands would be okay. Anne said it would be, but I kept second-guessing myself." He fixed his gaze on the monitor that reflected the baby's heart rate. "I don't know if Anne told you, but... I've never had a relationship, never even had a girlfriend before."

"You've never met anyone you liked?" she asked, a little surprised by that. David was older than she was, and she was practically an old maid. It was hard to believe that at thirty years old, he hadn't found a woman who wanted to be his girlfriend.

He shrugged. "I won't say that no one was ever interested in me, but I never pursued it. I always had this feeling that God had already chosen a wife for me. That I had to be patient." He grimaced. "That sounds cheesy, doesn't it?"

Bay laughed and squeezed his hand. "It sounds honest. And maybe a little cheesy," she teased to lighten the moment.

"All right," he said, pressing his free hand to his leg. "You're right. I should grab something to eat and make a couple of phone calls. I'm sure Matty is having a great time at Susan's house. They have eleven children. But it's still got to be scary. He's never been there without his mother."

"Take your time. I'll sit right here and wait," Bay told him.

He nodded.

Bay gazed into his eyes, then down at their entwined hands and into his eyes again. "You're going to have to let go of my hand for me to stay here," she pointed out.

They both laughed, and Bay imagined what it would be like to look into his eyes before she fell asleep every night and woke each morning. Suddenly, the idea of marriage was imminently more appealing and far less scary.

"All right, all right, I—"

"Bay Laurel Stutzman!"

The sound of Bay's name spoken from the doorway made them both turn around toward the door. Bay knew instantly who it was and she pulled her hand from David's as she leaped to her feet. *"Mam,"* she murmured.

Bay's mother wasn't looking at her. She was staring at David.

Bay hurried to her. "What are you doing here?"

Her mother held up a cloth satchel, slowly turning her gaze on her daughter. "I should ask you the same question," she replied, her voice low and terse. When Rosemary Miller got angry, she never raised her voice. She got quieter.

David rose from the chair beside Anne's bed and joined Bay. "You must be Rosemary," he said, offering a quick smile. "It's nice to meet you at last."

Bay's mother looked from Bay to David, then back to Bay. "I brought the two of you something to eat. Cafeterias are expensive," she said in Pennsylvania *Deitsch*. "I wanted to bring comfort to you and your friend, who

I can see is more than a friend. What are you doing alone with this man, Daughter?"

"*Mam*, David speaks *Deitsch*. I told you, he and Anne grew up Amish."

Her mother's mouth twitched into a frown. "Ham sandwiches, macaroni salad, grapes and cookies," she said in English, thrusting the bag at David. "Come with me, *Dochter*. Into the hall." It was an order, not an invitation.

"I'm sorry about your sister," Bay's mother said to David, her voice and posture stiff. "We will keep her in our prayers, my husband and I."

"*Danki*," David said. "For the prayers and the meal." He held up the bag she had handed him. "I appreciate them both, Rosemary."

Bay's mother gave a curt nod and walked out of the room, beckoning her daughter with a tilt of her head.

Bay considered, for an instant, refusing to go. She could tell her mother they would talk when she got home. But she realized that would only delay the conversation, and if she gave her mother time to heat up, it would go even worse for Bay that evening. So she gave David a quick look of dread, and walked out into the hall.

The brightly lit hospital corridor was a beehive of activity with men and women in colorful scrubs hurrying up and down the hall. There were people in hospital gowns, walking and pushing IV poles and wheeling in wheelchairs. And visitors, too, looking for the rooms of their friends and loved ones.

"What is it, *Mudder*?" Bay asked, using the formal term of address.

"*Aeckt net so dumm,*" her mother snapped, whipping around to face her. *Don't act so dumb.*

Bay groaned, rethinking her decision to speak with her mother while she was so angry. "Could we do this later? Anne is very sick. She's in heart failure. She might have to have an emergency C-section."

"For that, I am sorry, but *ne*, this cannot wait." Her mother stood nearly nose to nose with Bay. Folks were beginning to slow down as they walked by, curious about the two Amish women who were obviously having a disagreement.

"Can we at least go somewhere more private?" Bay tempered her tone.

She was angry and upset, and a part of her was afraid of her mother, or at least of the potential actions she could take. If her mother forbade her to be here alone with David at Anne's bedside, what would she do? She'd promised Anne she would be there for David, and for her. She couldn't leave the hospital. She wouldn't, she realized, no matter what the consequences. Not until she felt Anne and David would both be all right without her. But despite all of that, Bay didn't want to be disrespectful to her mother. Many years ago, when Bay was thirteen or fourteen, she had learned, from her mother, an important rule of dealing with others. No matter how much you disagreed with someone, it was never, ever right to be ill-mannered.

When her mother didn't respond immediately, Bay walked past her. "There's a lounge down here, where it isn't so noisy."

Her mother was silent until they passed a bay of elevators and turned into a small waiting room. It was set up with a couch, several chairs and end tables, and a TV mounted to the wall. To Bay's relief, there was no one else there. The TV was on, though, and she picked up a remote control and hit the red button on it the way she had seen David do earlier in the day.

"You lied to me, *Dochter.*" Her mother spoke half in English, half in Pennsylvania *Deitsch*, something she did only when she was very angry.

"I didn't lie to you." Bay settled her hands on her hips defensively. "When did I lie?"

Her mother crossed her arms over her chest. She was wearing a new dress of cornflower blue, a starched white apron, her best prayer *kapp* on her head, and new black canvas sneakers on her feet. "You purposely misled me. Misled all of us. You've been telling us all these weeks that you were seeing your friend Anne to help her out when you were sneaking around behind my back to see a man!"

"I *have* been spending time with Anne. *Mam*, she's been feeling poorly for weeks. I've cleaned, done laundry and looked after her son. I've even been cooking for the family."

"I'm glad that you've helped her, but that does not change the fact that you purposely did not tell me about this man. You are involved with him. I saw you holding hands!" her mother sputtered. "In front of anyone to see."

"We were alone in a hospital room, and Anne was asleep," Bay argued. "And I'm twenty-six years old! I have a right to choose who I hold hands with."

Her mother kept shaking her head. "Never in my life did I think I wouldn't be able to trust you, Bay. I thought I'd raised you better than to behave shamefully with a man."

"I've done nothing wrong with David!" Bay folded her arms over her chest, mimicking her mother's stance. "I care for him, and he cares for me."

Her mother's green eyes practically sparked with anger. "'Honor thy father and thy mother: that thy days may be long upon the land which the Lord thy God giveth thee,'" she quoted from Exodus. "Those are *Gott's* words."

"I'm old enough to make my own choices, *Mam*. That's why I didn't tell you about David. Because I knew you would be angry. I knew you wouldn't understand because you never understand me."

Her mother stood there for a long moment, looking at her, and Bay realized maybe for the first time ever that she was slightly taller. The observation was so unexpected that it caught her by surprise. Her whole life her mother had been bigger than she was, more imposing and always in control. And now, Bay realized, and she suspected her *mam* did, too, that her mother no longer had that control over her.

The thought was freeing.

But it was also intimidating. Bay's whole life, she'd had her mother, her father, then Benjamin and her siblings, and even her church to tell her what to do and what to think. And in a way, the control that she was fighting now had made her comfortable. It had made her feel safe. And now, standing here with her mother and defending her right to hold a man's hand, a man her family didn't know, she understood the dangers of making one's own decision. She was in uncharted territory here. Instead of having the wisdom of experience behind her, she was alone in her decision.

Would she leave her Amish life for David?

And once she made the choice she suspected she would, would it be the right one? Would her decision lead her to love and the freedom she yearned for or would it bring unhappiness and unfulfillment?

"You should have been honest with me," her mother said, bringing Bay back to the moment. "No matter what you thought my reaction might be, you should have been honest with me." She drew herself up, settling her black leather handbag on her elbow. "We'll talk about this at home." She started for the door. "I assume you'll be home this evening. That you're not spending the night here with *that* man."

Bay pulled a face in response to her mother's ridiculous implication. Holding hands with a man she cared for, especially a man who wanted to marry her, wasn't immoral. Her sisters had certainly done it with their husbands before they were married. But, of course, her brothers-in-law were all Amish. And that was all that mattered to her mother.

"*Ne*, I'm not spending the night here with a man," Bay countered, wondering what would make her mother say such a ridiculous thing. "I am going to stay here a while longer, though. The cardiologist said she would stop by at the end of the day. I want to hear what she has to say and see, when Anne wakes, if she needs me to bring her anything from home. Lucy said for me to call her no matter how late it was, and she'd bring me home."

Bay followed her *mam* into the busy hallway that smelled of antiseptic, cleaning agents and anxiety. It had been her experience that while, occasionally, something good happened in the hospital, like the birth of a baby, most patients were sick or injured. Feeling her own stress over Anne's illness, she could only imagine what others were feeling here, and not just patients and their families but their caregivers, too. It had to be such a weight on the shoulders of doctors, nurses and other medical personnel, looking after those in their care.

Bay stopped as her mother approached the elevator. "Aren't you even going to say goodbye?" she blurted.

Her mother turned around, speaking stiffly in Pennsylvania *Deitsch*. "Goodbye. I will see you tonight."

Bay took a breath as she tried to calm herself. She hated fighting with her mother. She loved her so much. She didn't want to worry or disappoint her, but she had to be true to herself to serve her family and *Gott,* didn't she? And didn't *Gott* make her who she was? And He didn't make mistakes. Wasn't it said in Psalms: As for God, His way is perfect.

Pressing her lips together, Bay willed herself not to cry at the state of her relationship with her mother. "Thank you again for bringing us something to eat. It was kind of you, coming all the way into town. We were getting hungry." On impulse, she gave her a quick peck on the cheek, something she didn't often do. Then she watched the elevator close, wondering if her relationship with her mother could survive if she left the church.

Bay stared out the truck window as they wound their way down country roads toward Hickory Grove. The sun was setting, leaving a glow over freshly planted fields and pastures thick with new clover. It was a warm evening, so she and David both had their windows down. Bay could smell freshly turned soil and hear the first sounds of night insects and frogs chirping and croaking.

She had stayed well past supper, sharing the homemade food her mother had brought with David, while poor Anne had enjoyed a meal of chicken broth and Jell-O. David got Matty on the phone, and after he and Anne spoke to him, she'd been surprised when David handed her the phone.

"He's asking for you, Bay," David told her.

The conversation was short, with her doing most of the talking, but Bay had been touched that Matty needed to hear her voice as well as his mother's and uncle's. It was interesting how important the boy had become to her in such a short time. On days like today when she didn't see him, she missed his smile, his laughter and the opportunity to read one of his well-worn Little House books to him.

After the cardiologist stopped by Anne's room to say there was no change in her heart function but that the drugs needed time to work, Bay had asked to borrow David's phone to call the driver for a ride home. But Anne had ordered them both out of her room, telling David to take Bay home and then stop by their friend Susan's to hug Matty for her. It was decided that Matty would stay the night with Susan so David could be back at the hospital in the morning to hear the doctors' latest reports.

Bay rested her arm on the open window of the pickup. "You didn't have to drive me home. I could have gotten the driver."

"I know I didn't have to bring you home." He reached across the bench seat and covered her hand with his. "I wanted to, Bay. After all you did for us today, it's the least I could do. I don't know what I would have done in the hospital today without you. You were so calm and asked such good questions."

She smiled at him. "You would have been fine." She glanced out the window again. "I feel bad, you taking me home when you still need to go back to your place to get Matty's nightclothes and his books."

David had decided that he should fetch a couple of Matty's books in case the boy got to feeling homesick. The plan was to take him the following day to see his mother at the hospital if she was up to it.

"After today, I needed this," David told her. "To be with you alone for a few minutes." He squeezed her hand.

Bay looked down at their hands entwined

on the truck seat, and she was amazed by how well they fit together. By how good his touch felt. She was scared to death for Anne. The cardiologist hadn't been all that optimistic the medicines were going to work, but somehow being with David made it all less scary.

"Are you going back to the hospital tonight?" Bay asked as they turned onto her road.

"You heard my sister. She said I wasn't." He cut his eyes at her, still steering the truck with one hand while holding hers with the other.

"But you're going back by, anyway."

He shrugged. "The hospital is practically on my way home from Susan's."

She chuckled. She had known that no matter what Anne said, David was going to check on her once more before he went home. Had Bay been in his shoes, she'd have done the same.

"Listen," David said. "I'm sorry about what happened today. Your mother seeing us holding hands. I shouldn't have…it wasn't appropriate."

"But I wanted you to hold my hand," she answered stubbornly.

He removed his sunglasses and tucked them into a small slot on the dashboard. "I take it you didn't have the chance to tell her about us."

"*Mam? Ne.*"

The shadows were lengthening quickly now. The sun had nearly set. She was afraid he was going to lecture her about why she should have said something before this, but he didn't. Instead, they rode the rest of the way to her house, holding hands in silence, both lost in thought.

When David pulled up in front of the farmhouse, she expected him to say good-night. They'd already made plans for her to meet him at the hospital in the morning, and she'd arranged a ride with Lucy. But he got out of his pickup and came around to walk her to the door.

"You should go," she told him, afraid he was going to want to come inside.

Then both her mother and Benjamin walked out onto the back porch, and she looked up at David, feeling as if she was walking into fire.

"There you are, *Dochter*. Home safe at last," her mother said. She wasn't smiling, but at least she wasn't scowling, either.

With a sigh, Bay spoke to her stepfather as she walked up the porch steps, "This is David Jansen, my friend Anne's brother."

She looked to David. "You've already met my *mam*. And this is Benjamin."

"Good to meet you, Benjamin. I've heard a lot about you." David offered his hand and Benjamin shook it, smiling.

"All good, I hope," Benjamin joked.

"All good. Bay sings your praises."

Benjamin glanced at Bay. "I know she's not my daughter, but I love her the same as I love my own. When Rosemary and I wed, we agreed we would share our children. Though there are some days I'd like to pass a few of my sons to her entirely," he said, looking to his wife.

Rosemary crossed her arms over her chest, saying nothing, and Bay wondered if this was all a huge mistake—considering marrying David and all that entailed. She had never seen her mother like this. Certainly her *mam* could get angry in the heat of the moment, but she had never seemed like the person who stayed angry. Bay had been sure that her mother would never shun her, no matter what, but what if she was wrong? Could she find happiness in a life with David if she no longer had her mother? And would Benjamin follow in her footsteps? Her brothers and sisters? Would they turn their backs to her if she ran into them at Byler's?

"Bay has been such a help to my sister, Anne, and me the last few weeks. And such good company for my nephew, Matty," David said, sliding his hand into the pocket of his jeans. "I don't know if Bay told you, but after my brother-in-law's death, Matty stopped talking." He looked at Bay with a hint of a smile, then back at Benjamin. "Bay got him back to talking when we couldn't. He adores her."

Benjamin smiled proudly. "Bay's got a way about her, doesn't she?"

David looked down, shuffling his feet. "I think you know now that I care for her, too." He looked up at Benjamin and then to her *mam*. "I want you to know that my intentions are honorable. But if you don't want me to see your daughter again, if you forbid her, I'll abide by your wishes."

Bay was so caught off-guard by David's words that she froze, her eyes widening. *He wouldn't see her anymore if her mother didn't approve?*

"*Forbid* her?" Bay's *mam* snorted. "If you think anyone could forbid that one from doing something, you don't know her as well as you ought to if you intend to continue seeing her." She turned to go back into the house. "You should come for supper when your sister is out of the hospital. Good night." A moment later, the screen door shut behind her.

Bay couldn't decide who she was more upset with at that moment, her mother or David.

"That's an excellent idea," Benjamin agreed, meeting David's gaze. "As soon as your sister is well, all of you should come for supper so we can get to know you better." He offered his hand. "Bark's worse than the bite with these Stutzman women." He flashed a smile as he shook David's hand, and then turned to the house. "A good night to you, David. And I'll see you inside, Bay. We're just about ready for evening prayers."

Bay waited until Benjamin went into the house, and then she marched down the porch steps. David followed her. "You won't see me again without their approval?" she demanded over her shoulder.

When he didn't answer, she strode toward his truck, determined to get an answer from him if it took all night.

Chapter Ten

David was surprised by Bay's anger. She was a spirited one, this woman of his. If she was his, and he hoped she was. Would be, he prayed.

"What about me?" she asked. When she reached the truck, she spun around to face him. "What about what *I* want, David? What would make you say such a thing to them? Don't you care what I think? What I want?"

He wasn't upset that she was angry with him. He knew Bay had to be worried about Anne and the baby. She and Anne had only been friends for a short time, but it seemed like a friendship that was solid and would be a long one. And nothing could please him more because, when he let his thoughts run wild, he imagined them all living in the big farmhouse together as a blended family—he and Bay, and Anne and her little ones.

"Why would you say that to them?" she repeated, crossing her arms the way she did when she was angry.

The funny thing was, he had seen her mother do the same thing at the hospital and again this evening on the porch. Bay thought she and her mother were opposites, but from his observations, they were very similar. Where did Bay think she got her stubbornness if not from Rosemary?

David took his time, choosing his response to Bay wisely. He didn't want her to be angry with him, but he had to be honest. It was who he was, and if she didn't like it, then maybe they weren't meant to be. "I said it because it was the right thing to do, considering the circumstances." He looked down at her, meeting her gaze. "If we were to marry, Bay, and have children, if we had a daughter, how would you feel about her seeing a man you disapproved of?"

"I would never forbid her!"

"And it doesn't appear your parents would ever do that, either."

Bay took a deep breath. "But if they did—I don't know if I can go against their wishes,"

she admitted softly. "Even if they don't forbid me."

"Wait. Are you saying you're considering
marrying me?" His chest tightened. All day
he'd been on such an emotional roller coaster.
It was hard for him to keep up with all he
was feeling, between his concerns for Anne
and the baby and his desperate need to have
Bay fall in love with him. He wanted her not
just to love him, but to be brave enough to be
willing to leave the life she had known for a
life with him.

He waited for her response.

"I'm saying—" She hesitated. "I'm saying I'm considering it. But I won't lie to you,
David. I'm torn." She pressed her hand to
her forehead. "Not about you. You're a good
man and we get along so well together. You
understand me in a way that no one here un-
derstands me." She took a breath. "It's me
I'm worried about. I didn't think I wanted
to marry. And be a mother?" she scoffed. "I
don't have a mothering bone in my body."

She was considering marrying him!

He smiled, deciding that while she hadn't
declared her love for him, her considering
marriage to him was good enough for now.
Because right now, she offered hope. "I'd dis-
agree with you on that. You're so good with

Matty. But because I don't want to be the object of your wrath again tonight, I'll say good-night. It's been a long day." He walked around the front of his truck. "Will you come to the hospital tomorrow?"

"Of course." She followed him to the driver's side, seeming calmer now. "I just wish I had a phone," she fretted. "In case you need me. I know Anne's going to be fine, but—in case you need me," she repeated.

"I can call the harness shop." He opened the door. He didn't want to leave, but if he didn't get moving, he wouldn't make it to Susan's house before Matty went to bed.

"But that's only during business hours. What if you needed me in the middle of the night?"

"Bay, she's going to be fine. The doctors have everything under control." He got into his truck. "She says she's cautiously optimistic." He frowned. "Besides, you're not allowed to have a cell phone. Are you?"

She closed the driver's door and leaned in through the open window. "Our bishop wouldn't like it. Of course, half the men I know have one. I know Jacob and Joshua both do. And Marshall and Eli." She frowned. "But, of course, they're men, and they need them for their jobs."

He lifted his brows. "Hit a nerve there, did I?" He chuckled, but she didn't. "I'm sorry, I shouldn't tease you like that, Bay."

She looked into his eyes and managed a smile. "Give Matty a big hug for me and tell him I'll see him tomorrow. Susan's going to bring him to the hospital to visit, right?"

"Yup."

"Okay, then. I'll see you both tomorrow." She waved goodbye as he pulled away.

As David drove down the long oyster-shell driveway, he couldn't help wondering what it would be like to kiss Bay. He had never kissed a girl before and now he was glad. Because, hopefully, Bay would be the first and last woman he'd ever kiss.

Bay stood in Anne's hospital room doorway and watched her friend as she read *The Deer in the Woods* to her son for the second time. Anne had steadily improved over the last week, and Bay and David felt better about her condition.

Anne had so improved that she was making tentative plans to return home, promising anyone who would listen that she would remain on bed rest. David wasn't thrilled with the idea, which Bay could understand. But she also understood Anne wanting to be home in her own bed to snuggle with her son each night and read him his favorite books.

Just in case his sister was able to go home, David had begun to make plans. He figured he could take care of his sister and Matty at night, but they were going to need help during the day with meals, cleaning, laundry and Matty, and Bay had volunteered. David and Anne's income was based on what he grew and sold, and he already had several big orders from a landscaping company, so he couldn't just take the month off until the baby was born. And once Anne had the baby, no one knew what kind of recovery time would be necessary. Bay had already talked to Joshua about only working weekends and early mornings at their shop and greenhouses. He had been very understanding, promising they would make it work, even if they needed to hire another employee, which they had been considering before Anne was hospitalized.

So far, the cardiologist had refused even to discuss the option of Anne going home. If anyone kept Anne from going home until it was time for the baby to be born, it would be the midwife, Julie, maybe because she knew Anne well enough that she doubted her patient would follow the rules of full bed rest.

Bay wasn't so sure Anne *wouldn't* comply; after all, she would be risking her own life or that of the baby's if she didn't. Her friend was such a good mother she would never risk her child's life. And with David at her side, watching her every move like the mother cat still living in their mudroom, she could see them making it work at home.

David walked into the hospital room as Anne finished reading a book to Matty who was snuggled into the bed beside her.

"You're back. Get your mysterious errand done?" Bay asked, smiling up at him.

When Bay arrived at the hospital, he and Matty were already there. He'd then excused himself, saying he needed to run an errand and left Matty in Bay's care. Anne had asked him where he needed to go, but he'd told her it was none of her bee's wax, which had made them all laugh.

"I'm back." David looked down at Bay, his smile meant only for her and she suddenly felt warm all over.

David slipped past Bay as Matty looked up at his mother with his big brown eyes. "Again, Mama. Read again."

Anne laughed. "Not again." She groaned theatrically and dropped back onto her pillow, making her son giggle. She was still wearing two heart monitors and had an IV, so there were wires and tubes everywhere. "I can't read it again."

Matty accepted the book and held it to his chest. "But I *wike* it," he told her.

She hugged him. "And I like it, too, but Mama needs to rest." She looked up at her brother and Bay. "And Uncle David is back. I think he and Bay have a little surprise for you."

Matty's eyes lit up and he turned to look at them. "S'prise!"

"We do have a surprise for you," Bay said. "Now give Mama a hug and come along."

Matty threw his arms around his mother, and she hugged him tightly again, kissing the top of his head. When her son pulled away, there were tears in Anne's eyes. "Thank you," she mouthed to Bay.

A lump rose in Bay's throat. If possible, she and David and Anne had all grown closer since Anne had been hospitalized. There was something about possibilities of new life and of death that made a person look past others' little quirks and their own worries and doubts to treasure the life God had given them. Bay was so thankful for Anne and David's friendship and for the possibility of a life with them both.

Bay had been at the hospital every day since Anne was admitted, even Sunday, to her mother's irritation, and she intended to continue coming. Bay didn't care how much it cost her to hire a van to bring her every morning or how far she was behind in her work at the shop. What mattered right now was Anne. And in being there for Anne, she was also there for David and Matty.

"We'll be back in two hours," David said as Bay lowered Matty from Anne's bed to the floor. "Get some rest."

"Take as much time as you like. Have some lunch while you're out. Matty needs to get plenty of fresh air. I want him behaving himself at Susan's and tired boys make well-behaved boys," Anne said. "I'll be right here when you get back, Matty." She raised her hands before lowering them to her rounded belly. "I've got nothing to do here. Nowhere to go."

"You've got something to do. *Rest*," David instructed.

Anne looked at Bay. "Please take my brother before I throw this book at him." She raised one of Matty's books he'd left on her bed.

Matty frowned. "No, no, Mama. No throw books," he told her sternly.

They all laughed, and then Bay, David and Matty left the hospital and walked down the street to an elementary school. Because school was out for the summer, Matty could play on the playground equipment. After taking turns pushing him on the swings, they took him to see a bright yellow slide. The first time he climbed the steps, he got scared, but Bay climbed up, set him in her lap, and together they flew down the little slide. Her *kapp* strings flying, she had found it exhilarating. They did it twice more, and then Matty took it solo. Then he was joined by two boys just slightly older than him, and their big sister, and Bay and David wandered over to a bench to sit and enjoy the June sun.

From the bench, they could still see Matty, and it allowed them to talk privately. Her favorite part of the day was when she and David stole a few moments to themselves. Sometimes they ate lunch together in the hospital cafeteria or waited in the little waiting room on Anne's floor while she had testing done. Sometimes they just sat together in her room, holding hands and whispering to each other while she slept. Had it not been for the fact that Anne was suffering from a severe condition, the days Bay spent with David would have been perfect.

"So," David said, drawling out the word. "Anne and I wanted to talk to you about something."

Bay could feel her brow furrowing. "What about?"

He put his hands together in his lap. Today he was wearing jeans and a teal-colored polo shirt. It was a brighter color than she was used to seeing on him, but she liked it. It made his green eyes seem even greener.

"Matty," David said. "Anne talked to Susan last night and then called me after I got home. Matty's been up at night crying for his mother." He shrugged. "Not unusual for a three-and-a-half-year-old. But Anne's worried about him staying so long. And she doesn't want to take advantage of Susan's kindness. She already has a house full of children of her own, and while she's a church friend, she and Anne aren't friends like, well, like you and she are. So we were wondering—and if this is too much, just say so," he added quickly. "But we were wondering if you would be willing to take him to spend the night with you for a few nights."

Bay didn't consider the question for a second. "Of course he can come home with me. I'd love that."

David smiled. "Anne knew you'd say that.

Matty loves you and trusts you. And we were thinking that if he can't be with us at night, at least he could be with you."

"I'd love to take Matty home with me. He'd have such a good time playing with my twin brothers. They're all about the same age."

He leaned on his legs, his hands still together. "But I know you've got work to do. We're getting into a busy season with retail."

She waved his thought away as if it was insignificant. "I can still work. He can go to the shop with me or hang out with Josiah and James. There are plenty of people around to keep an eye on them. You know how it is with a big family. Everyone takes turns with the little ones."

"But what about your mother?" David asked thoughtfully. "How would she feel about another mouth to feed? Because I know Anne is talking about coming home, but I don't see that happening. And the baby isn't due for another month. They want to get her as close to term as they safely can."

"*Mam* would be fine with me bringing Matty home," she told him, covering his hands with one of hers.

They held hands all the time now. Even in public, which she knew her mother would disapprove of, but Bay didn't see anything wrong with it. Not if she loved him. Which she knew she did, even if she wasn't ready to admit it to him.

"I'm sorry if I made her out to be a bad person, because she's not," Bay continued. "She's good and kind and I wouldn't trade her for any *mudder* in the world. She wants me baptized and married to a nice Amish man because that's what Amish mothers want for their children. She'll be pleased to know that you and Anne would trust us with Matty."

"Okay, so it's settled." He took her hand in his. "Anne will be relieved. I think she'd prefer he stay with you. We tried to figure out some way to have him stay with me, but she's afraid I can't get my work done. And if anything were to happen here and Anne needed me—" his voice filled with emotion "—I wouldn't want Matty here."

"David, everything is going to be fine. The medications seem to be working," she told him. "We have to trust in *Gott*."

He took a deep breath. "You're right. She's going to be fine. We just have to get through the next few weeks. And keep her in the hospital if we can." He turned on the bench so that their knees were touching. "So that's settled. Now, do you want to know where I've been this morning?"

"I thought it was none of my bee's wax," she teased.

"It was none of *Anne's* business because my sister can't keep a secret, and I wanted it to be a surprise."

"A surprise for me?" Bay asked.

"Yup," he said, pulling his hand from hers to reach into his back pocket. "If anything about this makes you uncomfortable, I can take it back. Not a big deal."

Bay frowned. "I'm not sure I like this."

"Who doesn't like surprises?" he asked, drawing his head back.

"Me."

"Well, I think you're going to like this one." He whipped his hand around to reveal what was clearly a brand-new cell phone.

"A phone?" Bay asked in shock. "You got me a phone?" She was so excited and yet she immediately tempered it. "No, David. It's too much. It's not appropriate. That's too much money to spend."

He looked into her eyes. "You think? Even for the person I love?" He lowered his voice to almost a whisper. "Because I do love you, Bay. You know that, don't you? Now, I don't expect you to say it back. Not yet. I'm willing to give you all the time you need. But I hope," he went on solemnly, "I pray, that someday you could love me. Even half as much as I love you."

It was all Bay could do not to say, *I love you, too,* but she held her tongue because she had to be sure she was willing to leave her church, her family, her life, no matter what the consequences, before she said the words.

She bathed in his gaze for a moment and then said mischievously, "Can I see it and then decide if I'll keep it?"

He laughed and handed it to her. "I didn't go fancy because I knew you wouldn't like that, but I got one that would do everything you need it to do—calls, messaging and the internet."

She closed her fingers around the phone, staring at it in awe. "A phone of my own," she breathed.

"So here's my reasoning before you hand it back to me telling me stubbornly that it's too spendy a gift." He glanced up, checking on Matty, and then returned his attention to her. "No matter when Anne is released, before or after the baby is born, we're going to need your help. Me calling the harness shop, trying to get a message to you, you calling me back, it's not working very well."

"Especially when Emily forgets to pass on the message."

He chuckled. It had happened the day before, though, thankfully, it hadn't been anything too important. He had just wanted her to stop at the house and get some clean nightclothes for Anne after he had forgotten them.

"And even if we can make the harness shop phone work during business hours, as you said last week, what about at night? What happens if Anne gets home and needs to go back to the hospital and I've got a three-year-old and newborn baby in my arms? I would need you to either go to the hospital with Anne or stay with the children."

Bay stared at the phone in her palm. Their bishop didn't permit it. If the bishop found out she had it, she'd been in trouble with him and the whole church. Living in a community that knew everything about everyone was one way they were able to keep their lives as strict as they did. A woman with buttons on a dress or a cell phone in her apron pocket would not only be gossiped about but would get a talking-to by every woman in her church district. She'd get visits from the preacher and other church elders and be pressured into a confession. It wasn't a place any woman wanted to be.

"I can't believe you bought me a cell

phone," Bay said softly. She looked up at him. "Thank you. But I want to pay you back."

"You'll do no such thing. I bought the phone because I need you to have one." Catching sight of Matty, he called out, "Sit down on the top of the slide! That's right, no standing." He looked back at Bay, who was swiping from screen to screen. "Does this mean you're keeping the phone?"

"I shouldn't," she said.

"But you will." He smiled at her. "You make me happy, Bay." He touched an icon on her phone that read Contacts. "I put my cell number in, the hospital number to Anne's room, and also our house number. I didn't know what other numbers you would want. Lucy's maybe, in case you need a ride somewhere?"

Bay couldn't stop touching the smooth, glass screen. It felt good in her hand, not evil, not even wrong. And her heart swelled as she looked at David, seeing her reflection in his sunglasses. It was on the tip of her tongue to just say it, to tell him that she loved him and that she wanted to marry him, no matter what. She was trying to get up the nerve when Matty cried out, not in joy but pain.

"Bay!" he cried in his little boy voice.

Bay and David were both on their feet instantly. Matty was crying as he clutched his arm, the big sister of the boys he had been playing with now standing over him. The children's mother ran toward them from the other direction.

"Matty, what's wrong?" David called to him as he hurried in his nephew's direction.

Matty was staring at the inside of his forearm. "Ow," he cried.

"I think he got stung by a bee," the little girl explained.

"Bay!" Matty sobbed as David reached him. "Want Bay."

Bay dropped her new phone into her apron pocket and scooped the little boy into her arms. "Oh, a bee sting. Can you show me?" she coaxed. "My poor Matty."

"Here," he sobbed, pointing to a red welt rising on his skin.

Bay bent her head to get a closer look, the little boy's tears wetting her full apron. "Oh dear, it is a bee sting."

"Owie. Hurts," Matty cried.

"Shhh," she hushed, pulling him close. "It's okay. We'll get a little ice for it. It won't hurt for long." As she held him and he wrapped his arms around her, Bay looked over his shoulder to see David standing there watching them. Smiling.

In that moment, Bay knew she would marry him. She knew this was God's plan.

Chapter Eleven

Bay glanced at the clock on the wall in Anne's hospital room. She and Matty had ended up staying the whole day to spend time with his mother. David had gone home for a couple of hours after Bay and Anne had insisted he need not be there every waking hour.

"It's almost time to go, Matty," Bay said. "Do you need to go to the potty before we get in the car?" She had arranged for Lucy to pick them up at seven. When David had gone home, he'd grabbed some clean clothes and toys for Matty, and of course, his precious books.

Matty nodded his head. He was seated on his mother's bed beside her, busy coloring in a book one of Anne's nurses had kindly brought him.

"Is it time already?" Anne asked. "I hate to see you go." She gave Matty a quick hug.

"Sorry, but I don't want our driver waiting for us in the parking lot." Bay rose from her chair beside David. "And Mama needs her rest, right, Matty?"

Bay was concerned that having Matty there all day had been too tiring for Anne, even though she had taken him for walks around the hospital several times. She worried that Anne was looking pale again, although Anne protested she felt fine.

"I can take Matty," David offered without looking up from his phone. "Just give me a second to finish this." He was using his cell phone to place an order for more hydroponic equipment. Even though he'd had little time to tend to it in the last two weeks, the few plants he'd planted were doing well, so well that he wanted to expand already.

"I don't mind." Bay picked up crayons Matty had dropped on the floor and placed them in the box.

"That would be nice if you'd take him, David," Anne said. "I need a minute alone with Bay."

Bay and David looked at each other and Bay could tell that they were wondering the same thing—what did Anne need to talk to her alone about?

"Um, okay. Not a problem." David looked down at his phone again. "And...order is placed!" He stood, sliding his phone into his back pocket. "Let's go, little man."

Bay picked up Matty from Anne's bed and lowered his feet to the floor.

"Here." Matty handed Bay the coloring book. He started to walk toward David, then turned back. "No *coworing*, Bay," he warned, waggling his finger at him. "My book."

"Hey, hey," Anne said, fighting a smile. "We share, right?" Shaking her head with a chuckle, she watched him walk out of the room with David. "He's going to have to get over being an only child, isn't he?"

"He'll be fine," Bay answered, tucking the last crayon into the box. "What did you want to talk to me about?" She slipped the crayons and coloring book into Matty's backpack and zipped it up.

"Come here." Anne patted the edge of her bed. "Sit with me."

Bay hung the backpack on her chair and sat down on the edge of the bed, surprised she didn't feel uncomfortable in such intimate circumstances. Anne was lying on her back in bed in a hospital nightgown, still hooked up to the monitors and an IV. With a house full of sisters and a twin, Bay was used to familiarity with them, but she'd never had a really close female friend before. She'd never slept in a bed or braided another girl's hair except her sister's. But sitting there beside Anne seemed…right.

"I wanted to thank you for agreeing to take Matty home with you." Anne took Bay's hand in hers. "It was very kind of Susan to keep him so long and I know he was safe with her, but he'd rather be with you. He loves you so much."

The idea that Matty loved her made Bay's chest tighten. "Like I told David, I'm happy to take him home with me. My little brothers will be thrilled to have a playmate their own age."

"I also want to thank you for loving my son," Anne went on. "Our *grossmama* always used to say that a child growing up couldn't have too many mothers."

Bay thought it was strange that Anne saw her in that role—a mother. But she was touched that she appreciated how much she cared for Matty. And Bay did love him. Somehow, the little boy had found his way under her skin. She didn't understand it, but she accepted it as well as her role as a temporary parent to Matty while his mother was in the hospital.

"You don't have to thank me. Matty is easy to love," Bay said.

"You might say the same thing about my brother," Anne teased, raising an eyebrow as she released Bay's hand. "How's that going? You two seem pretty cozy these days. I see you holding hands when you think I'm not paying attention."

Bay felt a warmth flush her cheeks. "You know, if David was here, he might say that was none of your bee's wax."

The two laughed together.

Anne was obviously not offended by Bay's teasing. "You know," she said, "David told me about the night he took you home and spoke with your mother and stepfather. It sounds like once this baby is born and I'm on my feet again, we might be joining your family for supper. If your church is like ours was, I'd think such a supper might lead to an official engagement."

Bay could feel herself blushing. "I don't know about that. I think Benjamin's idea was for the two families to get to know each other. And to appease my *mam*."

Anne was quiet for a moment. "Do you mean you're not interested in marrying my brother?" She held up her hand. "And I'm not saying this isn't a huge step, Bay. But would life be so different with David than an Amish man beyond electricity and a truck? You've seen how we live. Our lifestyle is simple, and church is still a very important part of our lives. God is still at the center of who we are."

"I know." Bay folded her hands in her lap, looking down. "I just want to be absolutely sure before I say yes."

"Sure that you love my brother or that you could go from being Amish to Mennonite?"

"Both." Bay looked at Anne. "I… I do have feelings for David, feelings I never expected. But I've only known him for two months. Is that enough time to know that you love someone, that you want to spend the rest of your life with him?"

"It can be. It was in my case. I met Matthew at a county fair. I was serving church dinners and he came in to eat. I ended up leaving my shift to walk the horse barns with him and ride a merry-go-round. Within hours, I knew that I loved him and that God had meant us to be husband and wife. And Matthew felt the same way. We had only known each other five months when we married."

Bay folded her hands together in thought.

"Can I ask you a question?" Anne said.

Bay nodded.

"You told me a few weeks ago that you haven't been baptized. Why not?"

The question took Bay by surprise. It wasn't something people outside their community asked. "We're not required to be baptized until marriage."

"It was the same in our church growing up. But you *could* be baptized without marriage plans. We knew several people from our congregation who were baptized and didn't marry until years later."

Bay thought a long moment before she answered, because she wanted to be honest with her friend and herself. She had told herself for years that she was putting off baptism because she didn't need to do it yet, but that wasn't the entire truth. "I wasn't sure… I'm not sure it's right the choice for me," she answered softly.

"Because maybe God had other plans for you?" Anne pressed.

"Maybe," Bay answered.

Anne sighed. "I'm not trying to put pressure on you," she said, meeting Bay's gaze. "But I don't want you to miss out if my brother is the love of your life. Do you love him?"

"I do," Bay whispered.

Anne smiled. "Then tell him. And then pray together asking God if marriage is what He wants for both of you."

At that moment, Matty burst into the room. "Candy!" he cried, a fun-size bag of fruit chews in each hand. "Goin' to share." He looked up at Bay. "*Wiff* new friends at Bay's house."

"I did not buy that candy," David defended as he walked into the room, his hands up as if in surrender. "Someone at the nurses' station gave them to him. And I got an extra so James and Josiah could both have their own." He held up a bag. "I hope that's okay," he directed to Bay. "I told him he had to ask their mother first."

Bay chuckled, getting up from Anne's bed, their private conversation over. "It'll be fine."

"Guess you better get going." David pointed to the clock on the wall.

Seeing that it was nearly seven, Bay looked back to Anne. "Get a good night's rest. We'll see you tomorrow."

Anne met her gaze. "Thank you for taking Matty. And for being my friend." She put out her arms.

Bay leaned down to hug her.

"Take care of my son," Anne whispered in her ear. "And my brother, too."

Bay pulled back to look into Anne's eyes that were filled with tears. "I will, but only while you're on the mend," she murmured. "You're going to be fine."

Anne hugged her one more time and then let go. "Come on. Kiss Mama, Matty. I'll see you tomorrow."

Bay lifted Matty onto the bed and Anne hugged him tightly, also whispering in his ear.

Matty struggled to get away, eager for his adventure with Bay. "Bye, Mama. *Wove* you."

"I'll walk you down," David said as Bay lifted Matty down and led him away. "Be right back, sis."

"I'll be right here. Where else can I go?" Anne asked.

By the time David had Matty strapped into his car seat in the hired minivan, it was after seven and the sun was slipping in the western sky. "See you tomorrow. Be good," he told his nephew, kissing the top of the head. "Can I talk to you for a second?" he asked Bay, closing the van door.

"Sure. I'll be ready in just a minute," Bay told the driver.

The severe-looking woman with close-cropped white hair put up her window and went back to reading her paperback book.

David took Bay's hand and led her a few steps away from the van to give them some privacy. "Anne tell you about her numbers?"

Bay frowned. "What numbers? No."

He drew his hand over his face. "I guess she didn't want to worry you. Her blood test results came back when you and Matty were down in the cafeteria having milk and cookies earlier." He looked into Bay's eyes, so thankful she was there to hear him voice his concerns. "She's not responding as well to the meds as she had been and there have been some irregular heart rhythms. The cardiologist has changed up her meds. If she doesn't improve, she may have to have the C-section sooner rather than later." The last words caught in his throat. He had stayed calm when he had heard the news because he didn't want to upset Anne, but she'd been surprisingly fine, insisting God would see Matthew's baby born safely. But inside, David was so worried about his sister that his fear was coming in waves.

"Oh, David," Bay breathed.

And then she surprised him by putting her arms around him, hugging him tightly. David slipped his arms around her waist. Feeling her in his arms brought a calmness no spoken words would have given him. The only bad thing about her hug was that he never wanted to let go.

"Bay," he breathed. "I wish I could kiss you." It came out of his mouth before he could stop it.

Her hands still on his shoulders, she drew back, looking into his eyes. "You know I'm not supposed to kiss any man but my husband." Her tone was mischievous.

"So agree to marry me. Then I'll *almost* be your husband and maybe I could have a little kiss."

Her green eyes danced in the fading light. "I didn't say you couldn't kiss me. And I wasn't looking for a marriage proposal. At least not tonight," she added.

With one arm still around her, David brushed the backs of his fingers across her cheek. And then, looking into her beautiful eyes, he kissed her gently on the lips. "How was that?" he whispered.

Bay's eyes fluttered and she touched her mouth. "I liked it."

He smiled down at her, wishing he could kiss her a hundred times more. "I'm serious about marrying you, Bay. Say the word and

I'll call our pastor tomorrow. I'll call him tonight if you say yes."

"I thought we were going to wait to make that decision, David."

"Does that mean you're still thinking about it?" He let go of her and took her hand. "Can I at least hope you're considering making me the happiest man alive?"

She smiled, her cheeks flushed. She was wearing a blue dress today and no apron, the strings of her prayer *kapp* tied at the nape of her neck. To him, there was no woman more beautiful than Bay.

"*Ya*, I'm considering it. I've been thinking a lot about what it would mean to leave my church, and I think… I think this is the direction God is leading me," she told him, speaking slowly. "We're raised to believe that our way is the only way, but I don't think I agree. I think that's why I was never ready to be baptized. Does that make sense?"

"To a man who wrestled with those questions ten years ago? It makes complete sense." He thought for a moment. "Maybe I should talk to my pastor about meeting with us. Talking with us about the possibility of the two of us marrying. He might have some good insight. He was raised Amish, too, though he left the order with his parents when he was a teenager. What would you think about that?"

"I think I would like that," she answered. "But we need to hold off until things settle down with Anne. Okay?"

He sighed. All she was asking was for him to be patient. He knew that wasn't too much to ask, but it was so hard because he loved her and he wanted to wake every morning to her lying beside him, looking at him the way she looked at him now.

"I need to go," Bay said. "But I'll see you tomorrow. I have a shipment of geraniums going out in the morning. After that, I'll come to the hospital. Hopefully, Anne's doctors will have some good news about the new medications."

"All right." He held up one finger. "But my marriage proposal stands. You say the word and I'll meet you at the altar."

"A church wedding," she mused. "I'd never considered that before. I always thought I'd marry in my mother's parlor."

"I'll marry you anywhere you want, Bay."

She smiled up at him and then hand in hand, they walked to the van and he opened the door for her. "See you tomorrow, Matty," he called, waving to his nephew.

"'Morrow." Matty blew him a kiss.

As Bay got into the van and buckled in, David had to resist the urge to kiss her good-bye. A stolen peck in the parking lot was one thing, but the beliefs he had grown up with about intimacy remained. He wouldn't kiss her in front of the driver or anyone else. Instead, he had to be satisfied with a quick squeeze of her hand.

"See you tomorrow," she told him.

"See you tomorrow," he echoed, feeling at that moment like the most blessed man on earth.

The following morning, while Bay waited for the delivery truck to take the trays of geraniums to a nearby gardening shop, she decided to make up some more planter pots. They sold out as fast as she could make them, and Joshua had told her that morning as she cut up Matty's eggs and sausage that they profited the highest percentage from her planters than any other item they were selling. That had surprised Bay, as they seemed so simple to make. She filled a big terracotta pot with potting soil, then planted flowers and greenery that complimented each other in color, height and texture. Sometimes she made one with a color theme, like with white geraniums, a spider plant and plenty of white vinca. Other times, she created planters in a burst of color like red, white and blue, which was always popular, especially around July Fourth. The fun thing was that no two planters ever looked alike.

While Bay combined New Guinea impatiens, blue salvia and pink petunias, Matty and her three-year-old brothers created their own flowerpots. Her sister Nettie had offered to watch all three boys so Bay could work, but Matty was more comfortable when she was nearby, so she'd taken them all to work with her. Bay's plan was for Matty to take the flowers he planted himself to his mother later in the day.

Josiah and James were making a large pot to go on their mother's front porch. While there had been a couple of blooms snapped off and some tears when Josiah had accidentally hit his brother's hand with the spoon he was using as a trowel, the project seemed to be going well.

The best part about their morning was that Matty was having a wonderful time. She'd never seen him so animated and he was talking nonstop with her little brothers. She loved seeing the three of them taking turns watering their flowers with an old plastic watering can they had found. As they played in the dirt, they chattered in little boy talk. While often Amish children didn't learn to speak English until they went to school because Pennsylvania *Deitsch* was spoken in the home, their parents believed it was important that their children be bilingual from birth.

Finished with the planter she was working on, Bay took a step back to have a good look at it, wanting to be sure it was properly filled in to allow for growth but also look good now. Satisfied with it, she began pulling through stacks of new planters, trying to decide if she wanted to do a shallow dish or another large one, when her mother burst out of the back door of the greenhouse.

"Here you are," her *mam* said, out of breath. "I've been calling you and calling you. No one knew where you were."

Bay stared at her mother, who seemed flustered, and her mother never got flustered. "Sorry, the boys were talking and… I didn't hear you with the greenhouse doors closed, I guess." She walked toward her mother, a terrible sentence of dread coming over her. "What's wrong?"

Bay's mother met her gaze. "David is here," she said, clasping her hands over her strawberry-stained apron. She'd been picking berries that morning, promising strawberry shortcake with homemade whipped cream for dessert that night.

"Oh." Bay had planned to meet David at the hospital later and wondered what was up. "Could you tell him to come on back? The boys aren't quite done with their—"

"Bay, you need to go to him," she said soberly. "He's out in the parking lot." She glanced at the boys, who had abandoned their project and were busy stacking plastic pots into towers.

Bay frowned. "What—"

"He needs you. Go now."

The look on her mother's face made her rush through the open door of the greenhouse, past the rows of flowers and vegetables and out the front door. She spotted David's white truck and saw him leaning on the back bumper, his head down. Lifting her skirt, she ran the last steps.

"David?" She stopped short in front of him.

When he lifted his head to meet her gaze, she knew. *She just knew.*

"She's gone," he murmured, tears running down his cheeks. "The baby's fine. A little girl. Born a little while ago." He smiled through his tears. "But Anne's gone, Bay. She went into cardiac arrest and they couldn't save her."

Bay felt as if her heart was shattering into a thousand pieces. *"Ne,"* she whispered, her own eyes filling with tears. And then she put her arms around him, and they held each other and cried together.

Chapter Twelve

As David went through the process of preparing to bury his sister, Bay remained at his side. She made phone calls, arranged to have Anne's burial clothing delivered to the funeral home, and rocked Matty to sleep in her arms as he clutched his favorite picture books. The hospital had agreed to keep the baby until after her mother's funeral. Afterward, David would have to bring home the healthy, seven-pound, red-haired infant, whom he had named Annie.

Three days after Anne died, she was buried in the local Mennonite churchyard. At the graveside service, the pastor had spoken words he hoped would comfort the congregation. "In my house are many mansions. I go to prepare a place for you." As he spoke, folks who had gathered tried to hold back their tears and come to terms with a mother taken to heaven before her thirtieth birthday.

Dressed in her black church dress and bonnet, Bay had stood beside David and listened to God's word, relayed by the somber pastor. Matty stood between them, holding both of their hands.

During the service, Bay's mind had wandered, and the pastor's voice had faded in her head, replaced by morning birdsong. Her gaze had shifted to the wildflowers growing along the line of woods beyond the cemetery, and she had lifted her face toward the sun to feel its reassuring warmth. She had wondered how the world could be so full of life when such a beautiful life had ended. She had sought comfort in the holy words and her belief in a life beyond the world she lived in and in Matty's small hand in hers.

In the days following the funeral, David's house was full of people wanting to help. Little Annie came home from the hospital and there was a limitless number of people from the Mennonite church and their family, many who had traveled from Wisconsin, wanting to hold her, make supper and help any way they could. But within two weeks, everyone returned to their lives. David and Anne's family went home, their church friends went back to their work and families, and the visits became less frequent, the casseroles fewer.

Two and a half weeks after Anne's death, Bay sat at the kitchen table with Annie in her arms as she tried to comfort the fussy baby. David had taken his youngest sister, Maggie, to the Philadelphia airport to return home to Wisconsin, where she lived with their older sister Ruth. Maggie, who had stayed after their family had gone, had been a considerable help to David in the days following Anne's death. She had cared for the children, keeping Annie with her day and night, and reheated meals and played and read to Matty. But now she was gone, and David would be alone in the house at night with his nephew and niece. Bay didn't envy him. Annie wouldn't be sleeping through the night for a while, which meant he would be doing night feedings.

That morning before breakfast, Bay had spoken with her mother about coming to David's every day to care for the house and children while he worked. Ironically, as his personal life had fallen to pieces, his business had taken off. He was selling his late brother-in-law's inventory of flowering bushes and fruit trees as fast as he could get them out the door. Several of his commercial clients had also expressed interest in his hydroponic experiment and offered to sign contracts even before David had produced his first fruits, vegetables or flowers.

Bay's mam had frowned as Bay explained her schedule for the coming week—how she would go to David's every morning and stay all day until after suppertime, when he would take over the children's care. Her mam had said nothing until Bay, impatient with her mother's attitude, finally asked, "Do you not think I should be there for him? Anne was such a good friend. How could I not care for her children?"

"I think it's good of you to offer to help, but he's going to need a plan, Bay," she had responded. "And it can't include you, a single woman, long-term. What will people think with you there all hours of the day and night?"

"Did you not hear anything I said?" Bay had asked in frustration. "I won't be there *all hours of the night.* Seven in the morning until six in the evening. Maybe seven if David is having a busy day." She had then lowered her hands to her hips, standing much the same way her mother was, and asked, "And how is this different than when Ginger was at Eli's *all hours of the day and nigh*t watching *his* children?"

Her mother's mouth had twitched. "Eli was a member of our congregation," she said finally.

"Ah, so Eli was Amish, and David isn't. Is that it? We should only lend a hand to Amish friends?"

"I don't know why you even ask my opinion," her mother had then said. "You're going to do what you want, *Dochter*, no matter what I say." She had then picked up the basket of dirty laundry at her feet and walked away. "At least take someone with you, James and Josiah, or one of your sisters so no one can say you're unchaperoned in a single man's house. One day I can come with you and we can do some deep cleaning. You said the little sister who had been staying with him wasn't much with a scrub brush."

Bay had just stood there watching her mother go, not knowing how to respond. Not knowing how she should feel.

Right now she was feeling overwhelmed. Annie was still fussing although she'd had a bottle and her diaper was fresh. Bay needed to start supper and she had clothes in the washer and dryer that she needed to take care of before David got home from the airport.

She also needed to collect the eggs from the henhouse and pick the green beans in the garden she meant to cook for supper.

Yet here she sat, cuddling Annie, breathing her precious baby scent and whispering in her ear that she was all right. That she would be all right because while humans didn't always understand God's way, He was good, and her life would be full of love and goodness.

Matty sat at Bay's feet playing with wooden farm animals as he leaned against her. He hadn't stopped talking after his mother's death, but he was clingy and cried easily. If Bay left him to fetch a diaper for Annie, he began to wail. He didn't want to be alone. And bedtime had become a nightmare for David. Matty cried incessantly for his mother and Bay, and it didn't matter how long David read to him; he didn't want to go to sleep. And just about the time Matty fell asleep from exhaustion, David said Annie would wake up, wanting attention.

Bay felt so bad for David. She didn't know what to do for him other than be there. Since Anne's death, they hadn't talked about anything personal, hadn't held hands. The romance seemed to be on hold. Which she knew was to be expected, because David was grieving and overwhelmed. He was taking life one day at a time, trying to do for his niece and nephew as Anne would have wanted. He loved Matty and Annie as if they were his own, and that was what kept him going. Which made Bay love him all the more. Though his sister's passing was still a fresh wound, he found a way to smile, to play with his nephew, and snuggle Annie close and whisper to her how much her mother and father had loved her.

Bay was grieving, as well. And as hard as it had been understanding her feelings for David, understanding this emotional pull toward these two children was harder. No matter how difficult her days here were, she wanted to be there with them. When she was home working at the garden shop, all she could think about was hurrying to finish so she could be with Annie and Matty. And David.

Though she and David hadn't spoken of marriage since the night before Anne died, she knew it had to be on his mind. It was on hers. But every time it popped up, she pushed it aside, afraid to contemplate the decision before her that had only become more critical with Anne's death. Because if David were going to keep Annie and Matty, as she assumed Anne would want, that would mean Bay would be marrying into an already-made family. With *two* children. And while her sister had found it easy to slip into Eli and his four children's lives, she wasn't Ginger. But she loved David and the children. That would be enough to make it work, wouldn't it?

The screen door slapped shut and Bay heard David's footsteps. She listened to him remove his shoes, and a moment later, he walked into the kitchen. The first thing she noticed was how tired he looked. The second was how handsome. Just seeing him made her heart skip a beat. How could she be so blessed to have this handsome, smart, wonderful man love her?

There was no denying she loved him. And over the last two and a half weeks she had thought long and hard about leaving the Amish church, and she had concluded she could do it. She knew her mother would be opposed, but she also knew her mother loved her and would accept her decision. At least eventually she would. So all she had left to do was to talk to David. Bay needed to tell him she would marry him and all of this worry and confusion she'd experienced over the last months would be over. The decision would be made.

"Sorry I'm late," David said, brushing his red hair off his forehead. He needed a haircut.

He'd been so busy the last month with Anne's hospitalization and then everything that had followed that he hadn't gotten a chance to go to the barbershop. She was amazed he could even get out of bed in the morning. Yet he did, and usually with a smile, albeit a sad one.

"The plane Maggie was taking out of Philly was late landing, and I didn't want to leave her in the airport until we knew her flight wasn't canceled." His sister Maggie was still Amish and had been raised by their oldest sister since their parents passed. She had come in a hired van with the family for the funeral, but she was flying home because she'd stayed behind.

David put out his arms, and Matty popped up off the floor and hurled himself at his uncle. David lifted him high in the air, and the little boy giggled.

Bay looked down at Annie in her arms. The infant was sound asleep, at last. Her eyes were closed, and she pursed her rosebud lips rhythmically. Getting up carefully so as not to wake her, Bay slid her into a battery-operated baby swing someone from the church had gifted. "It's just as well you're late." Bay hit the switch and gave the swing a small push. It began to swing steadily, making a sooth-ing clicking sound. "Supper's not even close to being ready. Clothes are wrinkling in the dryer and…" Her voice waned. She was tired. And sad. She missed Anne and she missed the idea of the life she had begun to envision with David as newlyweds without the responsibility of children of their own. At least for a while.

He waved his hand dismissively. "I'm not that hungry, anyway. And this one—" he set Matty on the floor "—he wants peanut butter and jam for dinner most nights. I give it to him. And there are leftovers from yesterday's supper." He stood there for a moment, hands at his sides, looking as lost as Bay felt. "Do you have to go yet? I had an unsettling conversation with my sister Ruth. I called her on the way home to let her know that Maggie was safely on the plane, and apparently, she and my brother Hiram have come up with a plan. Without any input from me," he added.

Bay didn't bother to look at the clock on the wall. David needed her. "I can stay a while longer. Want something to drink? I made lemonade. We could sit on the porch swing. Let Matty run around outside."

"What about this one?" He walked over to the baby swing, leaned down and planted a kiss on the top of Annie's hair that was so red that it looked like one of Matty's red crayons.

Bay watched David with Annie and felt a crushing wave of emotion. How was it possible that she could love this baby so much? And why did her feelings for David seem stronger since Anne died?

"Annie will be fine," Bay answered. "The window's open. You know how loud she cries. The neighbors half a mile away will hear her if she wakes."

He groaned. "Of course. You're right." He looked down at Matty, who was playing with his toys again. "Hey, little man. How about we go outside and play before supper?"

The boy nodded.

Five minutes later, Bay had put a leftover chicken and dumpling casserole in the oven to reheat and poured two glasses and one sippy cup of lemonade. Out on the porch, she found David seated on the wood-slat swing. Matty was out in the grass, playing with the mother cat and kittens that now spent part of each day outside.

Bay set Matty's lemonade on the steps for him and then passed a glass to David.

He patted the seat beside him. "Thank you for being here through all of this, Bay. I don't know what I would have done without you."

"Nonsense," she said, sitting down beside

him. "You had plenty of people here to help you—your sisters and brothers, all of your friends at church."

"Not the same thing," he told her, taking a swallow of lemonade before he set the glass on the table beside the swing. "They don't know me like you do. Like Anne did," he said quietly.

She wanted to argue that they were his family, but she understood what he meant. She loved her family, but right now, it felt as if David was the only person who really knew her. He was the only person who knew her hopes and fears and understood them.

She relaxed and lifted her bare feet as he put the swing in motion. "Tell me what your sister Ruth had to say." She had liked Ruth, who was ten years older than David, but the woman was rather rigid and had none of David and Anne's light-heartedness.

"She doesn't think I can take care of the children." David looked at her. His blue eyes were still the eyes she knew, but with a sadness that had taken hold after they lost Anne. "My brother Hiram wants to take Matty."

She frowned. "Take him where?"

"Adopt him."

"Adopt him?" she asked, her eyes widening

in disbelief. "But Hiram and his wife live in Ohio. How would Matty see you?"

"Oh, it gets better. Ruth is willing to take Annie off my hands."

Bay stared. "And she lives in Wisconsin! She'd separate Matty and Annie?"

He shrugged. "Ruth said that Hiram told her he could take Matty but not Annie. He said his wife wasn't willing to have another baby in the house. She just potty-trained their sixth child."

It was beginning to cool off with evening coming, but it was still warm and humid—a typical June day in central Delaware. She watched a honeybee flit from one white blossom of a buttonbush at the corner of the porch to the next. "What did you say?"

He exhaled. "Nothing. I was stunned. When Ruth said she had a plan to help me, I assumed she would offer to have Maggie come back and stay with me. You saw Maggie. She loved it here."

"She loved riding in your truck and flipping the light switch instead of lighting an oil lamp," Bay countered.

"Good point. But you know what I mean. And I'm not sure the Amish life is what she wants, and I thought that might be a way for Maggie to find out."

"But being Amish is what Ruth wants for her," Bay observed.

"It is." He shrugged. "I can't fault her. You know how it is with a big sister. They think they know what's best for everyone in the family. Even a thirty-year-old like me."

Bay sipped her lemonade. "You haven't met my older sister Lovey yet. She's pretty bossy."

He was quiet for a long moment and then said, "You probably already know this, Bay, but I can't let the children go. They're all I have left of Anne. And I don't think Anne would want them to leave here. I certainly know she wouldn't want her and Matthew's children separated." His voice cracked with emotion and Bay reached over and threaded her fingers through his.

She didn't say anything, though. Instead, she sat quietly and watched Matty lying in the grass, three black-and-white kittens climbing on him. The child's laughter rang in the quiet yard and she couldn't help but smile. Life really did go on, didn't it? Even after the tragedy of losing someone as dear as Anne.

"So," David said with a heavy exhalation, "it's time to have that talk, Bay." He turned to her. "I can't send Annie and Matty away. But I also know that Ruth is right—I can't care for them completely on my own. Not the way they deserve to be cared for. So, will you marry me? Now? As soon as it can be arranged?"

His question was so abrupt that it startled Bay.

"Will you take me to be your husband, take Matty and Annie to be our children?" he continued. "Because they will become ours. I know that. Annie never knew her parents and Matty... I'm not sure he'll even remember them when he gets older."

Bay fought tears, the sense of the children's loss washing over her.

"I know it won't be easy, but we can do it," David continued. "The two of us together. We can take care of these two and run this business. I could do it with you at my side and I think I could be a good father with you helping me. I don't know a thing about babies."

The way he said it made her bristle. He wanted to marry her so he would have someone to care for the children while he worked in the greenhouses. Was he just like everyone else? Did he think that the only thing she was good for was doing laundry and changing diapers? "I don't know anything about babies, either," she said.

"Sure you do. When I rock Annie, she

cries. When you do it, she goes right to sleep. Look at her in there right now." He pointed toward the kitchen. "Sound asleep. I can promise you she won't be doing that tonight when it's bedtime."

Bay felt a sense of panic building in her. She imagined Annie awake and crying in the middle of the night. She imagined herself awake in the wee hours of the morning, walking the baby, up at dawn making breakfast, working in the house all day long caring for the children. And never getting to work again at what she loved.

Was this what she wanted?

Before she met David, she had been sure of what she wanted, and more important, what she didn't want. She wanted to work in her greenhouses and run the business. She hadn't even been sure she wanted marriage and children. Fifteen minutes ago, she had wanted to tell David she would marry him. But was that because she really wanted to marry him, or because she felt sorry for him and the children?

She was so confused. Was she in love with David, or had she loved Anne so much that she would marry his brother to care for Anne's children?

"What do you think?" David asked. "Shall we get married?"

Bay felt a buzzing in her ears, and she pressed the heel of her hand to her forehead. She hadn't been sleeping well. She'd been going to bed late and getting up early. Burning the candle at both ends, that was what her mother called it.

David watched her. Waiting.

"I... I don't know, David," she said, not daring to look at him for fear she would burst into tears. "Can I have time to think about it?"

David stiffened. Bay still wanted to think about it? After all the time they had spent together in the last month, she still didn't know how she felt about him?

He felt sick to his stomach. It was time he saw the reality of his situation.

She didn't love him. She would never love him. It had all been false hope.

He had fallen for Bay so fast. So easily. But it hadn't been mutual. When he and Bay talked about marriage before Anne died, he had assumed it was her hesitation to leave the Amish church that was holding her back. Which he sympathized with because he had struggled with his understanding of his own faith, too. But apparently that hadn't been it.

She hesitated now because she didn't love him.

And that was what the *English* called a deal-breaker. No matter how much he loved and needed Bay, he would not marry a woman who didn't love him back. His parents had never been in love. Theirs had been an arranged marriage and though they came to respect each other and love each other in the way a family does, there had never been a romantic love. And the day David had left his black, wide-brimmed church hat on his neatly made childhood bed, he had promised himself he would only marry for love.

He rose suddenly from the swing, sending Bay flying backward. "You know what, Bay? You're right. That's a bad idea." His tone was so cool that he barely recognized it as his own. "It was a bad idea from the beginning."

She pushed out of the swing. "What?" She stared at him. "No, I didn't say that. It's only that—" She squeezed her eyes closed, then opened them again. "I'm so tired, David, and sad and I… I don't want to make a mistake that will ruin all of our lives."

He strode across the porch, away from her. "Matty, come on inside." He waved to the boy. "Let's get some supper on the table. Come on," he repeated when Matty didn't get up out of the grass immediately.

"David," Bay said behind him, her voice thick with emotion. "Please don't do this."

"Go home, Bay. Go back to your single, carefree life. There's no need for you to come here again. I'll manage with the children."

She darted around him, blocking his path to the door. "David, please, I only—" She exhaled, dropping one hand to her hip in anger. "How are you going to manage the children if I don't come back?"

"I'll get some of the women from the church. Susan said she had a niece looking for work as a nanny." He stepped around her. "Or Maggie can come back. Problem solved." When he reached the back door and turned to wait for Matty, who was now coming up the porch steps, Bay was still standing where he had left her. "Go home, Bay," he repeated. "I've got this."

Annie began to wail, the sound of her distress coming through the open windows.

"Inside, little man." David opened the door and pushed Matty in ahead of him.

In the kitchen, he lifted Annie onto his shoulder. She burped and he felt a warm wetness run down the back of his shirt. Tears filling his eyes, he hugged the infant, patting her back and whispering in her ear. "Shhh. It's all right, sweetie," he hushed. "Uncle David is here. I've got you, and I'm not going to let you go."

As he cuddled Anne's newborn, he turned to the windows and watched Bay get on her push scooter and head down the driveway. As she disappeared, he was choked with emotion, realizing that not only had he lost his sister but now he had lost the love of his life, as well.

Chapter Thirteen

That night Bay went to bed early without bothering to eat supper. Her *mam* must have sensed it wasn't a good time to question her, because when Bay announced she was going straight to bed, her mother gave her a quick hug but said nothing.

Bay slept so late the next morning that breakfast was over by the time she got downstairs. The kitchen was empty, except for her mother and James and Josiah. The sight of her little brothers immediately made her think of Matty and Annie, and she feared she would begin her day the same way she had ended the last—in tears.

Earlier, as she brushed her teeth and prepared for the day, she told herself that she had been foolish to think that things with David would ever work out. It had been a mistake to think that a man like him could ever love an unconventional woman like her. It was better it ended now. This way he could find the kind of woman he needed, one who would care for Anne's children, have a baby every year, and keep the house neat and clean, with meals on the table on time.

The talk she gave herself was a good one, so good that she nearly convinced herself that she was right, but by the time she made it downstairs, she could feel that she was on the verge of another good cry. After twelve full hours of sleep, she realized now that she'd made a terrible mistake. She *did* love David, and she wanted to marry him. She wanted to be a mother to Matty and Annie. But now she'd made such a mess of things. David had been her one chance at love and she had let it go. Let him go.

"Breakfast, *Dochter*?" Her mother was putting away the last of the clean breakfast dishes as Bay entered the kitchen.

Bay shook her head. "Just coffee. Where are Nettie and Tara?"

"Gone to Fifer's Orchard to see if there are any flats of strawberries. Tara wants to make strawberry syrup to add to her cache of jams." Her mother took a white mug from the dish rack and poured a cup of coffee.

"I can get it myself," Bay said.

"I know you can, but I want to do it for you. It doesn't matter how old a mother's child is, she still likes to do things for her. You'll feel the same way someday."

Bay dropped into a kitchen chair. "That seems unlikely now."

"Why do you say that?"

Bay didn't answer.

"Has something happened between you and David?" her mother pressed.

"We've broken up," Bay said softly. Tears filled her eyes as she reached for the mug in front of her.

"What happened?" Her *mam* took the chair beside her.

"I don't know. I guess we both realized I would make a terrible wife and mother. With David now having the responsibility of Annie and Matty, he needs someone who can do that. Someone who can cook and clean and be satisfied with that." Bay cupped her hands around the hot mug but didn't drink.

Her *mam* knitted her brows. "David said that?"

"Not in those words, but I know that's what he was thinking."

"Ah." Her mother leaned back in her chair, crossing her arms. "I've learned the hard way not to assume I know what people are thinking, not even those closest to me."

Bay stared straight ahead, saying nothing.

"Sounds to me like you're the one who's worried you'll be a poor mother." Her *mam* was silent for a moment and then went on. "You want to know what I think?" She chuckled. "Probably not, but I'm going to tell you, anyway. I think you would be a wonderful mother to Annie and Matty. I saw how you were when Matty stayed here with us and again at the funeral. He loves you and you love him. And that precious baby? I see the love in your eyes when you talk about her."

"But is that enough?" Bay's voice cracked, because she was thinking of David, as well. "I'm afraid it isn't."

"Of course it's enough. With love, you can do anything, including be a mother. Now, you might not be the mother I was to you, or the mother Ginger is to her flock, but *Gott* didn't create us to all be the same. I think, Bay, that you could be a different kind of mother than what you saw growing up. And I think you could be a good wife, just a different kind than I've been. You could be a wife who works beside her husband in their business. If anyone could do it, have a family and work, it's you."

Bay lifted her gaze, surprised by what she was hearing come from her mother's mouth.

"You know," her mother continued, "becoming Mennonite might be the way for you to find the independence you're looking for."

"Do you think so?"

"I do."

Bay couldn't believe what she was hearing and she stared at her mother. "But...but you were so angry when you found out I was seeing David."

"I was angry because you weren't honest with us. Because you were sneaking behind our backs."

"Because I knew you wouldn't understand. I knew you would never approve of the match with a man who wasn't Amish."

"And you were wrong." Now her *mam's* voice was laced with emotion, too. "You want a bigger world than the one you were born to. You always have. So I want that for you because all a mother wants is for her children to be safe and happy and to know *Gott*. You already know Him, and He will be with you, even on a pew in the Mennonite church."

Bay met her gaze. "You think I should marry David?"

"*Ya*, I do."

Bay sat there for a moment, stunned by

her mother's words. She wondered why they hadn't had this conversation weeks ago. "None of it matters now," she said, hanging her head. "Last night, David told me to go home and never come back."

Her *mam* got up from the table, shaking her head. "Well, it sounds like he can be as impulsive as you." She rested her hands on her hips. "Don't be stubborn, *Dochter*. If you love David and those children, fight for them. Sometimes you have to fight for love."

An hour later, Bay was busy transplanting dahlias, thinking over what her mother had said. Praying. She felt so miserable about the mess she had made with David that she didn't know what to do. Did she just go to him and tell him she was sorry and that she did want to marry him? Did she tell him she wanted them to have a marriage that was an equal partnership where they shared everything— work, the children, household chores?

Would he even listen to her now? What if he didn't love her? What if he'd only asked her to marry him yesterday to solve the problem with the children?

But she was usually so good at reading people. It had *seemed* like he loved her.

Bay was so frustrated and confused. She sat down on a tarp she'd laid out to keep from spilling potting soil all over the ground in the greenhouse. It was warm and humid inside and it occurred to her that she should open some windows or at least the back door. Instead, feeling so tired that she could have climbed back in bed, she stretched out on the tarp. No one would see her. Joshua was busy in the shop, tending to customers.

It felt good to lie down, so good that she told herself it would be okay to close her eyes for just a minute. She deserved it after the last month of running nonstop with not enough sleep. Just a minute, she told herself. Five at the most.

Bay had barely closed her eyes when she sensed someone was there. Someone had caught her napping in the middle of the day. Horrified, her eyes flew open and she found herself staring at Matty.

Matty? It had to be a dream. How would Matty get there alone?

"Bay, you *sweepy*?" Matty asked in his sweet little boy voice, squatting in front of her.

Startled, she sat up. It wasn't a dream.

"Matty, what are you—" Her gaze shifted upward.

Matty wasn't there alone. Of course he wasn't. David stood beside a table of potted dahlias, Annie asleep in his arms.

"David," she breathed.

"I see you found her," Bay's *mam* announced, strolling into the greenhouse.

"I did. Thank you," David said, seeming unsure of himself.

Bay got to her feet, looking from David to her mother and back to David again. "Tell me she didn't call you."

"I'm right here. I can hear you," her mother said as she put out her arms. "Give me that little one. Matty and I are going to find the boys, and I think Annie better help us."

"*Mam*, please tell me you didn't call him." Mortified, Bay covered her face with her hand.

"It's a good thing Rosemary did," David said, handing off the newborn. "Otherwise, I don't know how long it would have taken me to get the courage to come and say I was sorry."

"Matty, would you like to come with Rosemary?" Bay's mother asked cheerfully. "I think the boys are playing with our new kittens. Would you like to play with kittens with James and Josiah?"

Matty nodded excitedly, then looked back to Bay. "You wanna come *pway wif* kitties?"

Bay cut her eyes at David, then looked back at Matty. "How about if you go find James and Josiah and the kittens, and Uncle David and I will be along in a few minutes?"

Matty seemed to consider the suggestion before nodding.

"Come on, Matty." Bay's mother shifted the newborn to her shoulder and put out her hand to Matty.

David and Bay watched them go before being forced to look at each other when they were alone.

"Oh, Bay," David sighed, his arms slack at his sides. "I am so sorry. I don't know what happened yesterday. I was tired and worried and…and so sad." He adjusted his ball cap. "I was only thinking of myself and not you, not thinking about how stressed and sad you had to be, too. We both miss Anne so much. It was wrong of me to put that kind of pressure on you about marrying me."

Bay clasped her hands together, looking down at her bare feet. "No, I'm sorry. I think I took it the wrong way. I thought you were asking me to marry you so you could have a babysitter."

"What?" he asked in horrified surprise. "Bay, look at me."

She slowly lifted her head until they were eye to eye.

"I was *not* asking you to marry me so I

would have someone to watch the children. I can hire someone to do that. I asked because I couldn't stand the thought of you coming to the house every day and then leaving every night. I asked because since Anne died, I've felt so lost. I was afraid if I didn't ask you, you'd think that I no longer wanted to marry you because of everything that's happened."

As she exhaled, she felt a weight falling from her shoulders. "I'm sorry, too. I was tired, and then I got upset about Ruth and Hiram wanting to take the children. And then I... I got scared, David." Tears clouded her eyes.

"Come here." He opened his arms. "What are you afraid of?"

She went to him and rested her head on his shoulder. "That...that I won't be a good mother to Matty and Annie. That..." The warmth of his embrace gave her the courage to go on. "I was afraid, *am* afraid I can't be the mother the little ones need or the wife you want. I don't want to have twelve children. I don't want to spend every day in the house cooking and cleaning."

One arm still around her, he brushed a tear from her cheek with the pad of his thumb. "What would make you think I would want any of that from you? I want you to be happy, and I want you to be you. I want a wife who wants to be at my side, a wife who likes playing in the dirt like I do."

She gave a little laugh, sniffling. "I do like to play in the dirt."

"I can see now that I should have been clear, early on, when I realized we had feelings for each other, what I was looking for in a wife. What I dreamed our life would be. I want a wife who wants to work in the greenhouses with me, who can get as excited as me about cloning a fruit tree. I want a wife who can talk with our customers and take the truck into town to get groceries. I don't care if the house isn't perfect. I don't care about meals—I like macaroni and cheese from a box. It's what I've been eating since I left home ten years ago. And as for children—" he gazed into her eyes "—I know this wasn't what you had in mind, a newborn and toddler on the day you married, but more children? We'll make that decision together. And we don't have to do that anytime soon. If you ask me if I want children of our own, it would be a lie to say I don't. But Bay, I want you. More than I want more children."

"You want me," she breathed.

"I do. And just as you are. Feisty and independent."

She laughed and laid her head on his chest. He felt so warm, his arms around her so comforting. "But you told me to go home and never come back."

"I did. And that was a mistake. I was so upset about my sister and brother wanting to take Matty and Annie away from me that I thought they must not care about me. Not love me. And then when you said you weren't ready to give me an answer, I somehow made the ridiculous leap to think you didn't love me. Or the children."

"I do love Matty and Annie. I love them so much." She raised her head to look into his eyes again. "And I love you, David. And I want to marry you. And I don't care how messy it gets. I want to be with you for the rest of my life."

"Bay," he whispered, pulling her tight.

"Ask me again," she told him, resting her head on his chest.

"What?"

"Ask me again, David. If I'll marry you."

"Will you marry me, Bay?" he whispered in her ear.

She hugged him tightly, suddenly seeing the life she would share with him would be the life she had dreamed of. The life she had never thought possible. "*Ya*, I'll marry you, David. And no long betrothal."

"Because of the children," he said, holding her against him.

"*Ne*. Because I can't wait to be your wife." Then she kissed him, and knew in her heart of hearts that God would always be with them.

Epilogue

❧

Two years later

"Can you pour some water in this one?" Bay asked, showing Annie a planter she'd made with colorful dahlias and green herbs, something that was selling well at the shop she still owned with Joshua.

Annie toddled toward her, carrying a little pink plastic watering can. "Pretty," she said with a giggle, spilling water onto her dirty toes.

Bay laughed and carried a tray of basil to the potting bench David had built the winter before. "Keep pouring," she encouraged as Annie sprinkled water over the plants. "Mama will get you more water if you need it."

When she and David had first married,

she'd felt guilty referring to herself as Annie and Matty's mother, but as time passed, it had become second nature. At first, Matty had called her Mama Bay, but eventually, he dropped her name and their pediatrician had promised it was perfectly natural for him to call her mama. As time passed, while hopefully Matty wouldn't forget his mother entirely, his memories would fade and some might even be replaced by Bay's face, the doctor had explained. Bay and David were careful to talk about Anne regularly to both children so they would always hold her in their hearts, but the truth was that Annie had never known her birth mother. To Annie, Bay *was* her mother. And Bay felt honored and humbled by that each and every day. And blessed. So blessed.

"More *wawa*," Annie announced, holding up her watering can. *"Pwease?"*

Bay gave one of her red-haired daughter's stubby braids a playful tug. "More water? I can do that." She accepted the watering can and began to refill it with the hose. "Wonder what Papa and Matty are making for supper. Are you hungry?"

Annie was busy poking her finger into the wet soil in the flowerpot that was nearly half as tall as she was. "Hun-gry," she mimicked.

It was David's turn to make supper. After they married, they'd quickly realized that while it sounded like a wonderful idea to work in the greenhouses all day side by side, it wasn't always practical. No matter how much they and the children enjoyed the work, laundry still had to be washed, shopping had to be done, and meals needed to be cooked.

Now they worked together most of each weekday but set time aside for housework. It had been David's idea to share in the household and barn chores. He had no problem throwing a load of clothes into the wash before they sat down to have breakfast, which was often just cereal, or an egg-and-sausage casserole made the night before. And he was becoming quite the cook, with his sous-chef, Matty, at his side. So now, three days a week Bay and Annie made supper and three days a week David and Matty made it. Then once a week, they cooked together. Of course, sometimes one of them ended up with both children in the greenhouse or the kitchen, but that worked out fine because that meant the children received the attention they needed.

As Bay turned off the hose and handed Annie her watering can, Matty burst through the greenhouse door. "Supper's ready!"

A few steps behind him, David appeared

in the doorway. "Supper's ready," he called with the same enthusiasm as Matty.

Bay looked down at her daughter. "Sounds like supper's ready."

"Supper, supper, supper," Annie sang, abandoning the flowerpot to water her bare foot.

David walked over to where Bay stood and casually put an arm around her. He kissed her cheek. "How's it going?"

"Great." She plucked off her gardening gloves. "I've got five more flower and herb pots ready to go to the shop in the morning. How'd things go in the kitchen?"

"Just fine."

David kissed her again and she laughed, still learning his way with physical attention. "I thought as much since we didn't see any smoke?" she teased.

Marriage was nothing like what she had feared it would be. She was still amazed by how easily she and David had transitioned to married life and how right it had felt from the very first day. It had been surprisingly easy to move from the life of an Amish woman to a Mennonite one. While not everyone in the Amish community of Hickory Grove had approved of her decision, her family had embraced it with open, loving arms. And they had embraced David and the children with the same acceptance that quickly turned to love.

David gazed into her eyes. "I missed you."

She eyed him. "Missed me? You only went up to the house an hour ago."

He shrugged. "I still missed you."

"We made cheeseburgers on the grill," Matty told Bay. "And we put French fries in the oven."

Bay looked at David with surprise. "You guys cut up potatoes and made fries?"

"Of course not." He laughed. "But we did manage to open a bag of frozen fries. And there's fresh broccoli ready to be steamed in the microwave when we get up to the house."

"I guess we'd best go, then." Bay turned to her daughter. "Ready to have some supper, Annie?"

The little girl with eyes the color of David's looked up, beaming. *"Weady!"*

"Race you to the house!" Matty told David.

Before David could respond, Matty took off.

"Race? You want to race?" David called to his son as he ran after him.

"Come on, Annie!" Bay said, swinging her into the air and onto her hip.

Annie squealed with laughter. *"Wace!"*

Bay caught up to her men as they went through the greenhouse door and passed them outside in the grass.

"No fair," Matty cried. "You're bigger than me."

Then David lifted Matty onto his shoulders and Bay slowed to a walk. When David caught up, he reached out and took Bay's free hand in his. They made eye contact and he smiled.

"I love you," David said softly. "Thank you for being my wife. For making me the happiest man alive."

Bay gazed at him, her heart swelling with joy. "I love you, too. More every day," she told him, her eyes growing moist.

"Hey, I thought we were racing," Matty protested from David's shoulders.

Bay took off. "We are!" she called over her shoulder and both children burst into peals of laughter.

"Wait, no fair!" David called, running after them.

And side by side, Bay and David ran toward the house, sunshine on their faces, surrounded by all that was good and right in the world.

* * * * *

Dear Reader,

I hope you enjoyed Bay and David's story. I particularly liked seeing their friendship blossom into love. God really does have a place for each of us, even when we feel as if we don't fit in. We just have to be patient and willing to trust Him. I also think we need to learn to be open to possibilities. Bay thought she might not want to marry and have children, but she just needed to meet the right man! And wasn't David blessed to have found Bay? She truly was the woman he had been waiting for his entire life.

Thank you so much for spending a few hours with me in Hickory Grove. I hope we'll see each other again soon. Keep an eye out for me at Byler's Store!

Blessings,
Emma Miller

COMING NEXT MONTH FROM
Love Inspired

THEIR SECRET COURTSHIP
by Emma Miller
Resisting pressure from her mother to marry, Bay Stutzman is determined to keep her life exactly as it is. Until Mennonite David Jansen accidentally runs her wagon off the road. Now Bay must decide whether sharing a life with David is worth leaving behind everything she's ever known...

CARING FOR HER AMISH FAMILY
The Amish of New Hope • by Carrie Lighte
Forced to move into a dilapidated old house when entrusted with caring for her *Englisch* nephew, Amish apron maker Anke Bachman must turn to newcomer Josiah Mast for help with repairs. Afraid of being judged by his new community, Josiah tries to distance himself from the pair but can't stop his feelings from blossoming...

FINDING HER WAY BACK
K-9 Companions • by Lisa Carter
After a tragic event leaves widower Detective Rob Melbourne injured and his little girl emotionally scarred, he enlists the services of therapy dog handler Juliet Newkirk and her dog, Moose. But will working with the woman he once loved prove to be a distraction for Rob...or the second chance his family needs?

THE REBEL'S RETURN
The Ranchers of Gabriel Bend • by Myra Johnson
When a family injury calls him home to Gabriel Bend, Samuel Navarro shocks everyone by arriving with a baby in tow. His childhood love, Joella James, reluctantly agrees to babysit his infant daughter. But can she forget their tangled past and discover a future with this newly devoted father?

AN ORPHAN'S HOPE
by Christina Miller
Twice left at the altar, preacher Jase Armstrong avoids commitment at all costs—until he inherits his cousin's three-day-old baby. Pushing him further out of his comfort zone is nurse Erin Tucker and her lessons on caring for an infant. But can Erin convince him he's worthy of being a father *and* a husband?

HER SMALL-TOWN REFUGE
by Jennifer Slattery
Seeking a fresh start, Stephanie Thornton and her daughter head to Sage Creek. But when the veterinary clinic where she works is robbed, all evidence points to Stephanie. Proving her innocence to her boss, Caden Stoughton, might lead to the new life she's been searching for...

LICNM0122A